Moonshine Ridge Mountain Men Volume 2

The Joneses

Rocklyn Ryder

Magpie Press

Copyright © 2023 Rocklyn Ryder

All rights reserved worldwide
No part of this book may be reproduced, uploaded to the Internet, or copied without permission from the author. The author respectfully asks that you please support artistic expression and help promote anti-piracy efforts by purchasing a copy of this book at the authorized online outlets.

This is a work of fiction intended for mature audiences only. Names, characters, places, and incidents either are the product of the author's imagination or are used fictitiously. Any resemblance to events, locales, business establishments, or actual persons, living or dead, events, or locales is purely coincidental.

Retreat to the Mountain

About
Eddy Jones

Now that the rafting season is over, I won't need to leave Moonshine Ridge to go down to the big warehouse stores till next summer and that means doing more of my shopping locally.

Stepping inside the market, the bell on the door jingles, and I'm about to give Alice my customary greeting before grabbing a basket, when my head snaps back to the woman behind the counter.

The curvy brunette at the register is *not* the octogenarian store keeper that I've known my whole life and I know for a fact she doesn't belong to any of Alice's grandsons, the McAllister brothers, either.

Because this woman is *mine*.

Pepper's too young to have already suffered such big disappointment. She thinks her life is already over, but I'm here to show her that it's just beginning.

Welcome to Moonshine Ridge and the rugged wilderness surrounding the remote mountain community where the history is long, the local lore is deep, and the men are as wild as the mountains they come from.

Protective, possessive, totally obsessed; the men of Moonshine Ridge will do anything necessary to claim the women they love and give her the happily ever after she deserves.

The Moonshine Ridge books contain a lot of instalove, some swearing, some steamy scenes, zero cheating, and a lot of swoon-worthy happy endings. They're interconnected with recurring characters but can be read as stand-alones in any order.

Copyright © 2023 Rocklyn Ryder

All rights reserved worldwide
No part of this book may be reproduced, uploaded to the Internet, or copied without permission from the author. The author respectfully asks that you please support artistic expression and help promote anti-piracy efforts by purchasing a copy of this book at the authorized online outlets.

This is a work of fiction intended for mature audiences only. Names, characters, places, and incidents either are the product of the author's imagination or are used fictitiously. Any resemblance to events, locales, business establishments, or actual persons, living or dead, events, or locales is purely coincidental.

Chapter One

Pepper

Working at the general store here in Moonshine Ridge is a big change from the life I was used to.

Mid-September was when things started ramping up for another season of hard training and competition.

That's over with forever now though.

I stood on my last podium three years ago, with a gold medal around my neck, and the next winter Olympics in my plans.

One bad landing ended my career before I'd even graduated high school.

I spent the last three years in casts and braces. A couple of surgeries to pin my bones back together and a lot of painful rehab later only to get the official word a few months ago-- my career is over.

At twenty-one, I'm dusting soup cans in a small-town store for minimum wage a few hours a week, with no idea what I'm going to do with my life.

Kids I grew up with are off at college, they're getting engaged, and even starting to have babies now. They're all posting to their feeds their excitement about starting their lives. While I've spent the last three years coming to terms with the fact that mine is over.

At least, the life I expected to have.

I'm lucky though; I did well enough as a teenage competitor that I got some good endorsement deals, my parents had an insurance plan for me in case something like this ever happened.

Money isn't my issue. It's more of an existential crisis.

So when my dad said his old college buddy lived in Moonshine Ridge and Mike's mom needed help running her store, I knew he was telling me it was time to stop moping around the house and get back into the real world.

I grudgingly let my folks help me pack up my things and move me into a rented cabin on one of the residential roads that winds off of the main highway here in Moonshine Ridge, thinking I was coming up here to help out a doddering old lady.

Joke's on me there.

Alice McAllister is anything but doddering. She might be in her eighties, but she's got more of her wits about her than most people I know and it was pretty clear from our first meeting that she's the one doing *me* a favor.

She didn't really want help with the store. This is Alice's baby and she's been running it solo since taking over from her parents almost sixty years ago.

It's true though, it's been good for me to get away from home and all the reminders there of what I lost. Which is why I keep coming into the store for a few hours here or there, doing my best to do everything exactly the way Alice tells me.

This week Alice is letting me run the store by myself. She wasn't too happy about it, but her grandson is getting married this weekend and the whole McAllister clan is up at the resort at the end of the road for the week.

They aren't coming back till the rehearsal on Friday and Alice finally decided that it was worse to have the store closed all week than to trust it to me on my own.

I don't think that decision was about lost revenue though-- there seems to be some sort of feud going on between Alice and the lady that runs the museum across the street, Mable Hart. Apparently, closing the store for a week was going to give Mable gossip fodder and Alice didn't want rumors going around that she'd "up and died.".

FYI: running the only general store in a town the size of Moonshine Ridge at the end of summer when the campers and kayakers and Bigfoot hunters have left for the season? Boring.

A few locals pop in here and there to pick up the essentials or sometimes, the non-essentials like pop and chips or a candy bar or something. People are getting used to seeing me here, I've met most of Alice's family and I'm getting a fix on the locals.

But most days are just like today; dust, sweep, stack, check for bad produce and expired milk, rinse and repeat.

To be honest, without Alice here watching my every move, I spend a lot of the afternoon sitting on the stool behind the counter playing games on my phone and trying not to think too much about what I'm going to do with my life.

Eddy

It's been a while since I popped into Alice McAllister's general store. During the river season, my brothers and I take turns going down to the big box stores in Slow River to buy our supplies in bulk.

Rafting season ended with the holiday. The rafts are rolled up and put away for the winter along with the paddles and the life-vests and the helmets. Another summer's gone by and I'm already dreading the long winter ahead of me.

Up till a few years ago, the change of seasons was something to look forward to. I spent my whole life on the river and started working as a river guide for my grandparents' rafting business as soon as I met the insurance requirements. After we'd get everything stashed away for the winter, I'd turn around and start working for Bob and May up at the ski lodge.

Then Bob's health went downhill. He and May sold the lodge to a couple of city slickers that came up to the ridge with dollar signs in their eyes, thinking they were going to expand the old ski resort into the type of mega-resort you'd find in Colorado or down in Tahoe.

Those idiots didn't do any kind of research on Moonshine Ridge. Didn't know how small the place is; one hotel, one restaurant, one very tiny general store, and thirty miles of two-lane highway between us and Keller's Ferry that regularly gets shut down for days at a time by winter storms.

They managed to keep the place open for two seasons before the bank took it back.

Now the place is just sitting up there slowly rotting away because I'm the only fool dumb enough to want it-- working for the family business makes a decent living up here on the ridge, but it's a far cry from buy-a-ski-resort money.

So for the last few years, the end of the river season leaves me feeling more than a little lost.

Stepping inside the market, the bell on the door jingles, and I'm about to give Alice my customary greeting before grabbing a basket, when my head snaps back to the woman behind the counter.

The curvy brunette at the register is *not* the octogenarian store keeper that I've known my whole life and I know for a fact she doesn't belong to any of Alice's grandsons, the McAllister brothers, either.

Because this woman is *mine*.

She barely even looks up from her phone when she hears the bell on the door chime, and it kills me that she doesn't seem to even notice me.

I totally forgot what I came in for. I grab a couple potatoes from the bin, using my vantage point from the store's modest produce section to eyeball her from the other side of the stacks of Russets and yellow onions.

Thick waves of deep chestnut hair spilling over her shoulders as her head stays bowed over her phone.

I can't see her eyes from here, I can barely see her face; soft and full with skin unmasked by makeup. Her lips are full and a perfect shade of soft pink, made even brighter by the way her teeth are working into her bottom lip as she worries the phone's screen with her thumbs.

Her fingers tense around the device, her steady tapping going still and I think I catch her peeking up at me, shooting a quick glance in my direction through thick, dark lashes in a way that looks damn near dirty.

Quickly, I give up the attention I've been giving the potatoes and head for the aisle where the pasta is. Partly because I know how to boil pasta, and partly because I know it's the aisle dead center to the counter and I'll get another chance to study her.

She sets the phone down and pulls a magazine out from under the counter, leaning forward with her head propped on one hand and her elbow on the counter.

Cleavage creases deeply upward and the view I have of her creamy mounds pressed together above the V-neck of her feminine t-shirt has my dick threatening to embarrass me.

Her free hand rests near the edge of the page she's reading; short, pink fingernails tapping lightly against the Formica surface of the counter.

"Can I help you find something?" She asks, her sudden movement breaking me out of my daze.

"No, thanks." I'm an idiot. She just gave me an opening; I could have asked where the mayonnaise is or some dumb shit like that. "Been shopping here my whole life, I probably know the place better than you."

She raises one perfectly arched eyebrow while a corner of her mouth quirks up in an expression that is *not* a grin.

"OK," she tells me, skeptically. "Because you look a little lost."

Not any more, I'm not, I think as deep brown eyes meet mine over the boxes of cereal that line the top of the shelf between us. I just found exactly what I've been looking for.

Chapter Two

Pepper

Moonshine Ridge is a really small town. I've been working at Alice's store for a few weeks now and I thought I'd met all the locals.

This guy is new to me though. I definitely would have remembered seeing this guy around town.

He's got that surfer thing going on; corded muscles, zero body fat, tanned to the bone. With sun-bleached high-lights running through the light brown hair that's just long enough to flop to the side and give him a playful look despite the ubiquitous mountain man beard that all the men up on the ridge seem to favor, and a hard scowl narrowing his eyes.

Maybe the hard scowl just for me though. He's

been staring at me pretty hard since he came in. Not that I'm about to let on that I've noticed.

There's also no way I'm about to let on that I've noticed those muscles bulging under that sun-bronzed skin and the absolutely to-die-for forearms on full display in that white t-shirt with the blue logo on the breast that I can't make out from here.

No one should make picking out potatoes look that sexy.

I tap out a text with almost desperate speed, pulling a total creeper move and snapping a stealth shot of the mystery hottie to go with it.

Then I set my phone aside and wait for my friend, Hyacinth, to get back to me.

Hy works at the sporting goods place next door and she's married to Alice's youngest grandson, Ash. She adopted me pretty quickly when I arrived on the ridge and I'm sure that if she doesn't know who this guy is, Ash will.

While I wait for Hyacinth to get back to me, I grab a magazine from under the counter and try to look like I'm not totally perving on this guy with a thousand entirely inappropriate thoughts running through my head.

The magazine is Alice's. It's from AARP. So now I'm pretending to be totally into this article about fitness over fifty while taking every chance I get to sneak looks up at the dude who is currently studying the choices between thin spaghetti and boxed mac and cheese like there's going to be a test later.

This time when I dare one of my trying-not-to-be-obvious peeks up through my lashes, there's no mistaking the fact that he is definitely staring at me.

Feeling the heat of his gaze on me makes my insides flutter and I can't help but squirm on the stool I'm sitting on.

Hy still hasn't gotten back to me and I'm worried this guy is going to get away before I can find out something about him.

"Can I help you with something?" I sit up straight, doing my best put my boobs on display instead of my gut.

When I gained the weight after the crash, I got lucky, most of it went to my boobs and butt but my middle didn't escape the effects of a major lifestyle change that no longer includes a strict diet and hours of physical activity.

I'm still getting used to the new sizes in my wardrobe. But at least I have boobs now.

My voice echoes through the small store and catches us both off guard. I try to look confident, both as the person in charge of the store right now and as a woman.

One is easier than the other, to be honest, and I wish I could swap the two. Because when his Caribbean blue eyes lock on mine and everything inside me goes hot and wet? I wish I was the kind of woman who knew how to get a man obsessed with her.

He looks older than me but by how much is hard to tell. He could be twenty-five and prematurely aged by long days in the sun, or he could be forty and been careful with the sunscreen.

He's probably got a wife at home. Kids.

Ouch. The thought hurts more than seems reasonable considering I haven't even, technically, met the guy yet.

He probably just sees a dumb teenager that needs to lay off the carbs and take a few more hikes.

Not that I'm still in my teens, mind you. As of eight months ago, I am the proud owner of a snazzy new ID that lets me add rum to my colas over at Cedar's tavern down the street.

As for the extra curves? It might be true that my body's not in the peak condition it used to when I was a top competitive athlete but I can still hold my own on the slopes or the trails.

My physical therapists and my psychologist made sure of that.

Apparently, it was important for me to get back on the board even if I'd never compete again.

I snark off at the guy a little. It's not going to make me feel better but at least I feel less like a googly-eyed kid.

That's when he smiles. Right at me with his eyes locked on mine. His face breaks into a smile truly fit for a Hollywood star, full of perfect, white teeth, and full lips under the sandy blonde whiskers covering his face and I. Am. Gone.

Eddy

"Just in your eyes."

Yeah, it's a dumb-ass line and I know it, but I learned a long time ago that dumb-ass lines work when you deliver them right.

And it happens to be absolutely fucking true.

The dark, soulful eyes in question roll toward the ceiling but then I'm rewarded with a bright smile that quickly turns to a laugh that says she knows it's corny but she likes it.

"Smooth," she shoots back at me with a sarcastic grin. "Does that usually work for you?"

"Damn right it doesn't."

I toss a couple of packs of spaghetti noodles and a jar of sauce into my basket without taking my eyes off the beauty at the register.

"Well, I'm flattered that you think I'll be the exception to the rule," she retorts.

She's sassy. I like it. In fact, the more we exchange the banter, the more I like it. Her, really, the more I like *her*.

"No way. You're way too smart for the likes of me."

Making a quick round of the store, I toss a few more things into my basket; a bottle of wine, a loaf of French bread, a head of fresh garlic, a bouquet of the fresh flowers that Zephyr Hart grows.

A quick trip down the household goods aisle adds a couple of candles to the mix.

"Hot date?" She asks, spying the basket full of absolutely none of the things I had on my list when I walked in here.

"Yup," I pull my bank card out and prepare to tap it on the new point of sale interface that I see someone finally talked Alice into upgrading to. "Give me a box of condoms too-- extra, *extra* large."

Flashing her my best devilish grin, I lean over the counter and point at the green box hanging on the hook behind her. It gives me a chance to crowd into her space and I don't know if it's me or the condoms, but she blushes an absolutely gorgeous shade of pink that makes her olive skin glow.

"Lucky girl," she mumbles not quite under her breath as she scans the rubbers and tosses them into the bag with the rest of the stuff.

"Hope so," I mutter, looking straight at her.

My bravado's slipping, gotta admit. Up close to her like this, my attraction to her feels different than the usual flirtation. My dick's at half-mast and my lungs are full of the scent of vanilla and cinnamon from when I was close enough to get a whiff of her.

Wondering if it's body spray or lotion and if she puts it everywhere has my dick leaping to full attention, making me grateful for the old-style counter between us.

She gives me the total and I pay for the two bags of merchandise. My heart is beating fast and my palms are sweating enough that my card is slick from it as I slide it back in my wallet.

What the fuck is wrong with me? I've been picking up chicks since I was a teenager. It's never made me nervous before.

That's when it hits me; I really want this girl to go out with me.

No. Fuck that. I want more than a date.

This girl is different somehow.

"So, what's your name, anyhow?" I ask, making a point to lean across the counter just to breathe her in again as I reach for the pad of blank paper and the pen sitting next to the register.

"Pepper."

She watches me helping myself to shit on the side of the counter like I belong in her space-- truth is, Alice would wrap my knuckles with the flyswatter hanging behind the counter if she caught me doing this. But Pepper isn't Alice, not by a long shot, and I want to belong in Pepper's space.

"Nice to meet you, Pepper." I drop the pen on top

of the pad where I was just scribbling and grab my bags. "I'll see you at eight."

With my best smile, the one Mom always says no woman can say no to, I hand her the bouquet of flowers from the bag she put them in and head for the door, leaving the bells jingling as I let it swing shut behind me without giving her a chance to say no.

Chapter Three

Pepper

My mouth is still hanging open five minutes after the bells on the door go quiet.

When I look down at the pad of paper he was writing on, I see "Eddy J" and an address that I assume is his house.

Did he really just ask me out? Or, not "out," I guess, so much as "over."

Remembering the things he bought, pasta and sauce, wine, candles, bread and garlic; I mean it's pretty standard date night fare for a guy who plans to cook dinner for a woman. I just didn't think that woman was meant to be me.

The flowers he left for me are gorgeous too, a collection of larkspurs and some type of poppy wrapped with fragrant greenery and tied with one of the polka dot ribbons that Zephyr uses as her signature touch.

I bring them to my nose and inhale. The flowers are wonderful, but when my eyes close and I breath in deeply, what I'm really thinking about is the way *he* smelled. Manly; like soap and sandalwood and a personal scent that made my nipples pucker and my panties moisten in a way that I have never experienced before.

Ripping the sheet of paper with his address on it from the notepad, I fold it and stuff it in the front pocket of my jeans. Then I rummage through the storage shelves in the back room for a container, fill it with water, and set my flowers next to the cash register.

I've already entered his address into the map app on my phone and gotten directions. Too bad Moonshine Ridge is too small to earn a visit from the Street-view car, or I'd already know what his house looks like too.

Can I seriously do it? Can I go to his house and-- the box of condoms he had me throw in to the bag comes back to haunt me. They really were the extra-large ones too.

That might be faster than I'm ready to move.

Obviously, Eddy has more experience than I do and, judging by the cocky swagger he had as he walked out the door (not that I was craning my neck to watch him go, or anything,) he's not used to getting turned down.

My phone dings with a new text just when I about have myself convinced to go anyway-- I mean, what the hell? I'm twenty-one, it's about time I got some experience with guys anyway, and I've never met a guy that made me feel like I felt when Eddy was leaning over the counter so close to me I could have licked him if I wanted to. OK, I definitely *wanted* to! So maybe more like-- if licking strange guys was socially acceptable.

Right below my blurry shot of Eddy with a potato in his hand and a "who is this?" text to Hyacinth, her reply in all caps reads, "TROUBLE! STAY AWAY!"

All that excited anxiousness leaves my body in one long exhale.

Figures, I'd finally meet a guy that makes my blood tingle in my veins and he'd turn out to be toxic.

After a few more texts back and forth, Hyacinth has relayed enough information about Eddy Jones to have me rethinking taking him up on his invitation.

She's mostly just passing on what her husband, Ash, is telling her; the guys grew up together and they both volunteer for the local rescue and recovery team. I guess Ash knows Eddy well enough to tell me not to bother, he's not the kind of guy that plays for keeps.

I don't tell Hy about him asking me to come for dinner. I don't tell her how close I was to going. I sure as hell don't tell her about the condoms or how willing I was to find out if he really needs the extra-large.

Instead, I thank her for getting back to me and tell her to thank Ash for the info. I send her heart-eye emojis when she sends me a picture of her nine-week-old daughter sleeping on her daddy's shoulder and I re-confirm that I'll be going to the big family bash at the tavern this weekend for Birch and Maggie's wedding rehearsal dinner.

When six o'clock rolls around, I go through the check-list that Alice left me to do before locking up the door and flipping the sign over to "closed."

On my way home, I take a different route than usual. One that happens to go past the turn-off for Hummingbird Drive. I might turn my head and peer down the street as I pass by, but I don't turn and look for a house with the number 971 on the mailbox.

Instead, I head to the cabin I leased for the rest of the year that sits up on a hill overlooking the lake that borders the north end of town.

As I swap out my jeans and tee for a comfy pajama set perfect for Moonshine Ridge's chilly

September nights, I examine myself in the full-length mirror on the bathroom door.

It's just as well, I think, taking in the soft rounded contours of my body. As a kid, I was always scrawny, then I started skiing, then snowboarding, then competing, and I spent most of my life trying to keep my weight *up*. Between the major lifestyle changes from not competing anymore, and what my doctors assure me is normal metabolism changes as I edge into my twenties, keeping my weight up isn't a problem at all anymore.

Looking in the mirror is a harsh reminder that jacked as fuck guys like Eddy aren't in my league anymore.

He's probably one of those guys that just want to cross every new girl in town off his to-do list. There's no real chance it would have gone anywhere between us.

As I sit on the couch with a microwaved burrito and soda I didn't even bother to pour into a glass, I flip through TV channels and try to avoid noticing the time and all the thoughts of what could be happening right now if I'd made a different decision.

So, this is what it feels like to be a love-struck teenager with an impossible crush, huh?

Can't say I'm a fan.

Eddy

At the time, I told myself it was no big deal that she didn't show. I mean, it was a long shot anyway, right? She doesn't know anything about me except my name and address. I can't blame her for not going to a strange man's house for spaghetti with store-bought sauce and a night of sweating up the sheets riding my cock.

By nine o'clock, I knew she wasn't coming. And it's not like I left a phone number or anything. I can't be upset that I didn't hear from her. But I still am.

I'm upset that Alice is back minding her store and Pepper's been nowhere around for two days now. Moonshine Ridge is a small, and I mean *small*, town. It's hard to hide unless you're trying.

I know I can be over-the-top, but I don't think I'm scary, and from the way Pepper held her own when I was giving her a hard time the other day, I can't imagine she'd be hiding from me.

Walking into Ash McAllister's sporting goods store, I've got a mean scowl under the beard I'm already growing out for the winter and a ski with a broken binding.

"Hey man, what's up?" The man in question meets me at the counter when he sees me walk in.

"Need this fixed, for starters," I set the ski on the counter between us.

"Hi Eddy." Hyacinth, Ash's wife, greets me as she emerges from the backroom, bouncing their baby, Rose, in her arms.

"I can get this done by next week," Ash tells me, setting the ski against the wall behind him, "what else ya need?"

Now, don't get me wrong, Ash is my buddy and all. We grew up together and we've been working together on the volunteer rescue and recovery crew since we graduated high school.

The thing is, Ash found his woman up on the river. Just last summer, he left one of his brothers in charge of the store and went up to do some fishing. Then he comes back with this curvy little redhead who's head over heels for him.

Now, it's not like I'm attracted to Hyacinth or anything like that, but the river is my turf. I've been running those waters since I was a tyke, sitting in grandpa Jones's lap while he let me help paddle the canoe. Damn near thirty years now, that river has been my home, and Ash McAllister goes up for a fucking weekend and comes back with the love of his life.

And I guess I feel like maybe he owes me one.

"What's Pepper's story?" I jerk my thumb backwards, in the general direction of his grandmother's general store but it's not like he doesn't know exactly who I'm talking about.

"Pepper's story is she's out of your league." Ash's

voice wavers somewhere between good-natured buddy and protective dad. "She's too good for you, too young for you, and I already had Hy warn her off from you. So don't bother trying to chase that tail, man."

Hyacinth looks between her husband and me with interest, but Rose starts to fuss in her arms and she excuses herself to go in back and take care of the baby.

"How fucking young is she?"

I mean, I knew Pepper was young, but she was minding the store by herself and she sold me the wine.

"She's twenty-one, I think," Ash tells me.

My head swivels toward the back of the store where Hyacinth just disappeared into the back room.

"You're one to fucking talk, jackass." I'm keeping my voice down, but I'm not in a joking mood anymore. "What's Hy? Nineteen now? Married, with a baby already and she's not even old enough to buy alcohol yet. What are you? Twelve years her senior?"

"Hy's different," he growls at me, "I love Hyacinth. Knew I wanted her beside me till the day I die the moment I saw her. I wasn't just out to notch my tent-pole with a pretty tourist. Hyacinth is my forever girl."

Silence hangs in the air between us as we glare

at each other. My jaw is tight enough I can feel a muscle twitching on one side of my face.

"Hey, Eddy," Hyacinth's soft breaks our staring contest as she rejoins us. "You know we're doing Birch and Maggie's rehearsal thing at the tavern tomorrow, why don't you come down?"

Ash turns to give her a suspicious look.

"What? Most of the other recovery crew guys are going," she tells her husband with feigned innocence and a sweet smile.

"I'm surprised you weren't already planning on being there." She turns back to me with that same innocent smile and I don't have to be hit over the head to catch on to what she's really saying.

Pepper will be there.

"Actually, yeah, now that you mention it, I was planning on going. Thanks for reminding me, Hy," I give her a smile and then shoot another glare at Ash, "I guess I'll see you tomorrow night then."

On my way out the door I can hear Ash asking why she would invite me like that and I'm not quite out of hearing range when she tells him I'm in love with Pepper.

It's enough to bring my feet to a sudden stop as I reach the sidewalk outside.

Is that what this is? This fixation I've had on her since my first glance at her? The way I can't get her off my mind. It's one thing that I can't stop picturing her naked and wet and screaming my name, but I also find myself picturing her with her belly round with our children. I want her curled up beside me at night and I want her eating meals at the table with me. I want her on the river with me all summer, I want her on the slopes with me in the winter. I want her growing old with me while we raise babies into grown children and I want to spoil grandchildren with her.

Holy shit.

I *am* in love with Pepper.

Chapter Four

Pepper

It was nice of the McAllisters to invite me to the big rehearsal dinner. I know my dad and Michael go way back together, but the only thing Mike promised to do for me was get his mom to let me help around the store to give me something to do. I never expected the McAllisters to include me in so much of their family stuff.

They've been really kind and it's nice to have people who are almost as good as family when I'm so far from home.

Besides myself, Hyacinth has also managed to adopt each one of her sisters-in-law; Maggie and Cami, so I also won an instant circle of friends when I arrived in Moonshine Ridge.

That's been amazing. I had friends before, but

they were always friends from the teams I competed on. At first, after the accident, there were lots of people coming by the hospital or the house after every surgery. Lots of texts and phone calls and flowers and balloons and "can't wait to have you back" well-wishes.

When my recovery took longer than expected and I had to withdraw from the team and finally, from competition altogether though-- the people I'd considered friends started to disappear from my life.

I'm still in touch with a couple of the girls, but only because we follow each other on social media. We never talk anymore, just "like" each other's posts.

I may only have been in Moonshine Ridge for a few weeks now, but something tells me Hyacinth isn't the kind of woman that lets her friends fade out of her life. She's got the kind of personality that draws people to her and she cherishes the connections she makes.

Which is probably why she's turned out to be the center of our still-forming girl group, even though she's the baby of all of us.

Of course, she's also the only one of us that already has a baby, and Cami and I were throwing rock/paper/scissors for turns holding baby Rose until Violet showed up with the mysterious McAllister brother, Cypress, in tow.

Now no one gets to hold Rose but Cypress and

all the women's hearts are melting watching the huge, gruff mountain man cradling his tiny niece in his arms.

"How long are you and Birch going to wait to start trying for your own?" Hyacinth comes up from behind where I'm standing with Maggie and Cami as we all stare at the baby that's being so rudely hoarded away from us now.

"We never aren't trying." Maggie snorts and we raise our glasses and clink them with hers.

The liquor is flowing freely tonight, thanks to Cedar and Cami, who run the tavern where the private family event is going on tonight.

Except Hy-- I guess there are some weird rules that allow her to drink under twenty-one since she's married to someone of age, but she's breast-feeding, so her glass is filled with ginger-ale.

Since Cedar owns the tavern and the lodge connected to it, anyone who doesn't have a sober driver tonight has a free room waiting for them. One of the perks of planning the wedding after the end of the summer tourist season-- plenty of empty rooms at the lodge.

When we're done toasting to Maggie's healthy sex-life, she runs off to join her soon-to-be-husband, Birch, and Hyacinth and I heckle Cami for a while. She and Cedar just got together officially after playing the grumpy boss/employee game all summer.

I missed most of that, but Hyacinth assures me the only ones they were fooling were themselves.

"Hmm," Cami's eyes drift off the baby to the man in the kitchen that we can see preparing food for all of us through the window in the wall. "Cedar wants all the babies now," she says with a dreamy little smile that makes Hyacinth swoon.

A wave of pure jealousy slams into me, though.

Cypress returns the sleeping baby Rose to Hy's arms, muttering something about having to find Violet. It's pretty obvious that the last McAllister brother is off the market now too.

Not that I'm interested in landing one of the dark, brooding, McAllister boys. No. My heart is stubbornly stuck on a certain, sandy-haired, sun-bronzed Adonis with a Hollywood smile and an A-frame cabin that backs up to the river running behind the row of houses on Hummingbird Drive.

So, I may have taken an exploratory route on my way into town the other day when I met Hy and Cami for lunch.

Since Alice hasn't let me near her precious general store since she came back early from the family vacation up at the Diaz's resort at Serenity Springs.

Speaking of Alice and her primary accomplice, Marcia Diaz, they are both in their early eighties and they are both snockered. They've been seriously doing shots of whiskey at a table in the back since before I got here and it sounds like they are plotting some kind of revenge on someone.

"Do not even listen in on that." Hyacinth's voice is a warning as she herds me away from the old ladies and their conversation. "I'm sure it would only make you an accomplice to whatever it is they are plotting."

"Your glass is getting empty," she nods toward the tumbler in my hand with nothing but a few half-melted chunks of ice left in it. "Why don't you head in back to the bar and get a refill?"

"What are you up to?" There's a glint in her eye and smirk on her face that tells me I'm likely to find more in the bar than just another whiskey and cola.

"Nothing," she shrugs, careful not to disturb the sleeping baby in her arms, "but you know, Ash is back there with the guys from the rescue and recovery crew...the *whole* crew."

My eyebrows lift into my hairline. Hyacinth winks at me.

"He's *here?*" I whisper frantically, shooting a nervous glance toward the hallway that connects the main restaurant to the bar in back.

"Just got here. He went through the back."

Hy knows all about my ridiculous crush on Eddy Jones now. It took exactly one night of steamy sex dreams for my crush to outgrow my ability to keep it to myself. My lunch date with her and Cami the other day was pretty much them lending support while I cried into my root beer float and chili-cheese fries.

"When were you going to tell me he was coming tonight?" I hiss through my teeth as she grins at me. "Oh my gosh, do I look OK? What do I say to him? Are you sure he even wants to see me again?"

"You look fine and you should say something witty like, 'Hi, I've had sex with you fifteen times in my head and I'd like to find out if you live up to my expectations.' "

Hyacinth's gaze goes over my shoulder and she adds, "And you should be ready to say it now."

Eddy

"There's my ghost pepper," I say as I walk up behind her.

Hyacinth immediately makes herself scarce.

Pepper spins around to face me. Her eyes are wide and her skin is that pretty pink color from the blush that lights up her cheeks and runs all the way down to her cleavage.

I'm not going to pretend I don't notice the deep crease between her full breasts and the way the creamy flesh peeks over the plunging neckline of the soft, blue sweater she's wearing tonight. Or the way those globes start to rise and fall more quickly with her shallow breathing when I step up close enough that I can almost feel the tips of her puckered nipples brushing against my chest.

Fuck, she's perfect. From the thick, dark hair falling down her back, to the curves filling out that sweater and the tight jeans that cling to her shapely legs like paint till they disappear under a pair of knee-high boots.

But it's looking in her eyes that has me unspooling like a dropped ball of yarn inside.

Pepper is mine.

I know it beyond a doubt as I stare into her wide, chocolate eyes and the realization hits me that I knew it from the second I saw her.

"Ghost pepper?" She asks, "Is that because I'm so hot?"

That little quirk of the corner of her mouth gets me. It takes every ounce of will power I have not to kiss the hell out of her right here and now.

"That too," I concede, "but mostly because you ghosted me on our dinner date the other night."

A look flickers over her face and I wish I hadn't brought it up. I don't want her to feel bad about that. I don't want this beauty to feel bad about anything.

"Yeah, I was going to but--"

"But Ash had his wife cock block for him," I finish for her.

That blush creeps up her neck again and has me wondering how far down it goes.

"Apparently you have a reputation on the ridge," she chides playfully but I can feel a more serious question under it.

"I'm a man reborn since I met you." It sounds like another cheesy line but damn if it's not the truth.

Not touching her is killing me and I'm sure if I lay a hand on her in here there's going to be four drunk McAllisters hauling me out back. Apparently, they've kind of adopted her as the baby sister none of them need.

She laughs at my line but those thick eyelashes flutter as she looks up at me through them and I can see the hope in her expression.

"Let's get out of here," I say, "before Alice and Marcia are drunk enough to get us in any real trouble."

"I came with Hy and Ash," she tells me, apologetically.

"Yeah, I think Hyacinth expects you to ditch her. We can walk to my place from here if you want."

She gives me a smile and a nod.

I wait by the door while she goes to find Hyacinth to let her know she's leaving.

Maggie comes through asking if anyone's seen her cousin, Violet, and I hear Pepper's voice calling out to let her know she found her. A few minutes later, Pepper slips her hand into mine as if it's something we've been doing our whole lives, and we walk out the door just as we can hear Alice shouting at someone to give her a ride to Mable Hart's place.

"The McAllisters are so nice," Pepper says, curling herself against my side as we walk, "but they are crazy."

"My family's worse," I tell her. "Here." Stripping off the lined flannel I have on over my t-shirt, I stop and hold it so Pepper can thread her arms into the sleeves.

"Worse?" She laughs, "Worse than drunk old ladies with a vendetta?"

Flannel or no, I'm not giving up an opportunity to wrap my arm around my girl and hug her tight against me.

"You should have seen them when Ash and Hyacinth got hitched." I shudder in recollection. "My grandpa Don literally had to call the sheriff. They hiked up to the storage yard and were trying to harness one of the canoes to a couple of goats."

Her shoulders shake under my arm as she laughs, "so your grandpa had to have the sheriff come get them?"

"No, Grandpa Don called the sheriff to stop Vera from shoving the lot of them into the river."

"Who's Vera?"

"My grandmother," I answer. "Vera's tight with Mable Hart and Mable and Alice have had some kind of feud going on since they were all in high school together back in the fifties. Things get crazy when any of them get together."

"Hyacinth says your grandparents started the rafting company back in the sixties?"

I love the way her arm snakes around my waist, but her hand has managed to find its way under the hem of my t-shirt and the soft touch of her fingers as they run up the bare skin of my back has my dick jealous enough that it's getting uncomfortable to walk.

"Yeah, Vera and Don were genuine hippies. Did the whole tour the states in an old school bus thing and then decided there really is no place like home. So they parked the bus on the old mining claim land from when my great great great grandfather Mel first found gold here and starting charging tourists for rides down the rapids. Built up the business, traded the school bus camper for a proper house once they were on baby number two. Mom and Dad took over the rafting outfit about five years ago after Don dislocated a shoulder trying to push a kayak out of a bad section of class fours."

"So that tan is from being on the river all summer?"

I chuckle as I steer us up the front walk to the A-frame cabin set far back off the street. "More like from being on the river my whole life," I tell her, as I lead her through my front door. "About the only time I haven't been on the river, I've been on the slopes. Till the ski lodge went bankrupt a couple years back, that is."

"What about you, Pepper? What's your story?"

"Ash didn't tell you about me?"

I flick on the lights and watch her look around my place. It's not big, just bedroom upstairs and the open floor plan with the kitchen and living room here on the main floor. We'll need to find something bigger for the plans I have for us.

"Are you kidding? Ash barely stopped threatening to kick my ass for asking you out."

"Yeah, Hyacinth thinks you're in love with me."

She turns to face me and she looks so fucking cute standing in the middle of my living room I'm ready to fall on my knees and beg her to marry me already.

My flannel is about ten times too big for her, hanging down to her knees and the sleeves well past her hands. Her hair is pulled over one shoulder and she plays with the ends, absently twisting them between two fingers as she looks back at me with half a smile that I can't quite read.

"I am," I tell her honestly. "Does that scare you? Is it too much too fast?"

Her head shakes back and forth lightly and the half a smile perks into a full one.

"No."

Chapter Five

Pepper

He's serious.

I can already tell the difference between kidding around Eddy and the Eddy that's standing just a few feet away from me, looking at me like his life depends on my approval.

The craziest part is that I feel the same way. When I look at Eddy, I see so much more than a hot guy that makes me want to do all the things I put off for so long while I was chasing Olympic dreams.

I see all new dreams in those cobalt eyes. I see more than dreams; I see my future.

That should scare the living daylights out of me but instead, I'm turned on.

An insane kind of turned on that has me rushing to meet him halfway as our bodies collide in a tangle of hands desperate to touch each other everywhere all at once with our lips sealed together.

Eddy's tongue moves against mine, twisting and pulling till I'm moaning into his mouth.

The flannel shirt he let me wear home hits the floor. His hands are on my breasts, kneading them over my sweater till I can't stand the teasing anymore. I unhook my bra and push his hands under my clothes so that I can feel him against my bare skin.

When his thumbs brush my nipples, I gasp. I had no idea it would feel so good to have a man's hands on me like this. I want more.

His shirt slides over his head and he lets me pull it free from his arms before returning his attention to my breasts.

Eddy is every bit as ripped under that shirt as I imagined he would be. My hands graze across rounded shoulders and along the indention where deltoids meet bulging biceps before starting a new mission to map his chest with my fingertips.

When my hands dare to drag lower, after tracing the six pack of abs that are stacked like bricks, down his flat stomach where I brush the tip of his erection where it pokes out of the waistband of his jeans, the game gets serious.

"Upstairs." Eddy's voice has lost the playful tone. It's darker and gruff as he growls the command against my neck where he was just sucking hard enough to leave a mark.

Taking my hand, he leads me up the staircase to a loft bedroom with windows stacked to follow the triangular wall looking out on the darkness of the river.

Eddy bends to unzip my boots for me and then he reaches up, undoing my jeans as if he was unwrapping a present and exhaling slowly as he peels them down my legs.

"Fuck, baby, you're amazing," he whispers before planting a kiss against my belly. He presses his face into the space between my legs and his hands wrap around the backs of my thighs.

The way he groans against the sheer fabric covering my mound is so sexy I feel the space between my legs going from damp to wet. My clit throbs and I thread my fingers into his hair, pulling him into me shamelessly.

"Your pussy smells like heaven, baby," he says, breathing against my clit through my panties till I can feel the moist heat of his breath.

"Let me feel you." His hand moves up the inside of my leg from my knee, along my thigh and I have to take a step to widen my stance so he can work his finger all the way between my legs.

When they reach my core where wetness is pooling, he inhales sharply and groans again, his finger brushing delicately across the crotch of my panties at first and then delving beneath the fabric and sinking inside of me.

Now it's my turn to groan, my fingers tightening in his hair with his head still between my legs as he kneels on the floor before me.

As he sinks a finger from one hand deep inside me, his other hand pulls at my panties till he has me exposed and then he leans in and puts his mouth on me.

Stars explode in my line of sight. I have no idea what I'm saying and no control over it. I'm vaguely aware that my nails are clawing at the back of his neck as he pushes one broad shoulder between my thighs and forces my leg over.

His arm is holding me, keeping me braced in a grip so strong that I know he'll never let me fall. So, as he suctions over my clit while he pushes a second finger deep into my slick channel, I know it's safe to let go.

When my vision clears and the roaring noise leaves my ears, Eddy kisses me where my body is sensitive from the orgasm, making me shiver all over.

"Incredible," he mutters, "fucking incredible, baby."

With less urgency, he rises to his feet and strips both of us all the way bare before leading me to the bed where he climbs into the middle and pulls me with him.

"You're so fucking tight," he tells me, "When you were coming it felt like my hand was in a fucking vise. I can't wait to feel you come on my cock."

Eddy

She's laying on top of me with her soft curves pressed against my naked body. I can feel the heat of her flushed skin over every part of me and I swear my cock is harder than it's ever been before.

Her hands wander along my jaw, stroking my beard, and tracing my collar bone.

"I want that too," she purrs against my chest as her lips run a string of kisses over my pecs. "I just need to go slow, OK? I'm not really sure if it's going to hurt or not."

With a laugh, I roll her over and land on top of her, teasing myself by pressing my hard length into her slick folds.

"Baby, I'm big, but I'm not that big. You're plenty wet, you feel that?" I reach between us and stroke her pussy from opening to clit and back. "Fuck girl, you're so wet for me baby."

"Yeah, but I've never done this before."

I'm not sure I heard her right. I'm not sure I would hear anything right, so much of my blood is in my throbbing dick right now, I think I might be hallucinating.

"What do you mean? Never done what?"

I can feel the tip of my dick leaking pre-cum, adding to her wetness and sending tingles up my spine as I draw the broad head along her seam again with nothing but the promise of heaven on my mind.

"Never had sex," she whispers tentatively even as her fingers dig into my arms and she spreads those thick thighs even wider to beg me into her body.

What she's saying registers somewhere in the part of my brain that's still civilized. I stop teasing at her entrance and look in her eyes. Really look.

There's desire there, every bit as urgent as my own, but there's something else too. Fear?

Shit.

This is fucked up. I can't just push my way into her sweet little body like some greedy, rough animal.

Pepper's choosing me to be her first and that's something that deserves some fucking gratitude, not a hard, raw fuck in the middle of the night after we've both had a couple of drinks.

Rolling off her, I gather her in my arms and hold her close.

"I'm sorry," she finally says, her breath warm against my chest. Then I feel the wetness of tears where her face is pressed to my skin.

"Hey." I look down and pull her chin up so she looks back at me. "Uh uh, no crying, baby girl. Why are you crying?"

"I didn't want you to stop." Her lips trembles as she fights to hold back the tears, "I shouldn't have said anything."

"Oh, hell no, that's definitely the sort of thing I want to know."

"But now you're having second thoughts about me, aren't you?"

Her voice gains back some of the confidence I'm used to hearing and she struggles to push herself out of my grasp.

"Fuck no!" I'm almost shouting as I pull her back against me. "Fuck no, I'm not having second thoughts. Not about you, not about us, not about the future I plan to have with you, or how bad I want to fuck your virgin cunt till it's molded to my dick forever."

She chokes a bit and coughs when I say the rude words but that doesn't seem to be what's offended her.

"So why did you stop?"

I sigh deep and relax a little when she lays her cheek back against my chest, her fingers drawing designs in my chest hair.

"I don't know; I guess I'm thinking that we both had a couple drinks tonight, it's already late, you're probably tired, and maybe a fast, hard fuck with a mountain man river bum you just met isn't the way you always pictured your first time. Even if that river bum is so obsessed with you that he never plans on letting you go."

She shrugs under my arm. "I was into it."

To prove her point, she wriggles out from under my arm and down my body, laying hot kisses along the way. Her hand wraps around the root of my cock and strokes me up to the tip.

All the muscles in my thighs tighten as I pump into her hand. Then she licks the slit, lapping at the pre-cum there before taking me in her mouth completely.

"Pepper, baby," I grit out on a low moan, "be careful, that thing's loaded, it's likely to go off without warning."

She laughs with her mouth still wrapped around me and the vibration of it has my hands fisting in the sheets to keep some kind of control.

"Tell me if I'm doing it right." She pops her mouth off me to speak, giving me a chance to breathe again.

"You're doing it right," I pant, "are you sure about this?"

"I want to make you feel good, Eddy." She seals her lips over the head of my dick and slides down my length again until she gags and the feel of her throat constricting around me has me seeing stars but when she comes up for air again and looks up at me with those pink lips swollen and wet from sucking my dick, I'm in danger of going off like a fountain in her hand.

"And since you won't fuck me, I guess I have to settle for this."

Once, during a high-water year when the river was feeling particularly mean, a kid got bucked out of the raft when no one was expecting it. I moved pretty damn fast that day to grab his life vest and haul him back in the boat before he got swept downstream.

Right now, the lightning quick reflexes I had that day look like a three-hundred-year-old tortoise taking a nap compared to how fast I have Pepper on her back with her knees bent back to her chest as I push into her beckoning heat.

Fuck, she's wet. She's hot and she's tight as hell but there's no resistance as I slide all the way in till I'm bottomed out inside her and I don't give either of us a chance to adjust before I'm pulling back and slamming in again. And then again.

Pepper's fingers claw at my shoulders and then I feel her nails rake down my back so hard I might be bleeding, but it's not a plea for me to stop or slow down. If anything, my naughty girl is egging me on with soft cries of "more," and "yes," and "harder."

My ears are full of white noise and my vision is tunneled down so the only thing I see is Pepper's face; those brown eyes wild with the storm raging through her, her lips parted on a silent oath, as her body accepts every thrust as I pound into her in a feral frenzy.

Her hips move to meet mine and then her teeth catch her bottom lip and bite down, her hands move down my back till she's gripping my ass and pulling me into her and holy shit, watching her come undone on my cock is the most beautiful thing I have ever seen.

Pepper arches her back, pushing those gorgeous, full tits up against my chest where we slip against each other from the sweat drenching both of us.

Her body tenses and then the tight tunnel my cock is sheathed in clamps down hard and starts to pulse. I don't stand a chance. My cock fucking erupts inside her, pumping jets of sticky seed into her unprotected womb till my balls are empty and I swear they're still twitching when I collapse against her.

Chapter Six

Pepper

My body feels languid, I'm lying on Eddy's bed with his body weight pressing me into the covers we never bothered pulling back, but I feel like I'm floating on clouds.

A pleasant buzz continues to light my nerves and I am deliciously sore between my legs.

As our breathing slows and returns to normal, Eddy repositions himself and pulls me tightly against his chest. Kissing the top of my head and then my face when I look up at him before finally sealing his lips to mine in a slow kiss.

"Shit baby, did I hurt you?" His eyes are wide with worry and his hand trails down and caresses my bottom.

I don't want to freak him out.

"Maybe a little," I confess, "not like I thought it would, more like, I'm just sore now."

"Sorry baby, wait here."

Gotta admit, not a fan of Eddy untangling our bodies so he can climb out of bed and disappear into the master bath.

"Here, take these." Eddy returns with a glass of water and a couple ibuprofen tablets. I struggle against exhaustion to sit up and swallow the pills as Eddy climbs on to the bed and moves back between my legs with a very soft, warm, wet wash cloth.

"Shh," he soothes as he takes the water glass from me and sets it on the nightstand. "There's some blood. You're sure I didn't hurt you?" He looks genuinely concerned.

I shake my head against the pillow under it.

"Felt amazing," tell him, not able to hide my grin one bit, "five stars, will ride again...after a nap."

He answers with a short laugh but my eyes are already closed and I'm fighting to stay conscious long enough to drift off in his arms.

He fusses with the blankets, getting me underneath them instead of on top of them, and then the light goes out and I feel him hovering over me beside the bed.

"You want something to eat? More water?"

"You," I tell him, making the effort to reach my heavy arms up to grab him around the neck and pull him down to me. "You, bed," I mumble sternly at him, "I need you to play pillow."

I get another chuckle and a kiss on the head and then he climbs in under the covers beside me and we curl up together; my head on his chest and his arms circled protectively around me as if we've been sleeping like this for years.

I drift into happy dreams of Eddy cradling babies in his arms.

"So, you haven't been on the snow since?"

When I woke up this morning, Eddy was already out of bed. He left me a towel and some of his clothes to change into and I found him downstairs in the kitchen singing very loudly and very off key when I emerged from a long, hot shower.

I've been filling him in on how I ended up in Moonshine Ridge.

"Yeah," I correct, accepting the warm blueberry muffin he just pulled from the oven. "It was part of my therapy after all the surgeries and then the rehab. They wanted to make sure I didn't develop PTSD or something, so I had to get back on the slopes as soon as I was cleared by the physical therapist."

"But you didn't like it?"

Eddy's pretty typical of a lot of guys I knew back

in the day, on the river all summer and then switching to snow for the winter. Or, at least, that's what he used to do until the ski lodge a few miles past town shut down permanently a couple of seasons ago.

He's been so sweet and understanding as I unravel my tale for him, but I can see the disappointment in his eyes. That look that tells me that he feels like he has to make a choice between me and his dream to reopen the lodge someday.

I move to the automatic coffee maker and fill a mug, taking my time to answer.

I don't want to be the reason he doesn't follow his dream, but I don't think I can share it with him either, and that's the sort of thing that can make or break a good relationship.

Eddy

The weather down in town is still pretty nice today, but storms moved into the high elevations overnight and I got reports from my brother, Current, that there's already over a foot of fresh snow higher up.

I've lived in these mountains my whole life and I still get a kick out of how crazy the weather can be, with sun down here and winter storms already moving in just a thousand feet higher.

I was hoping Pepper would be up for a day in the snow with me, but that suggestion opened up a pretty deep conversation.

She's already had so much disappointment in her life, losing her chance of competing in the Olympics, for fucks sake. Not to mention all the physical pain she went through; a year of surgeries to pin broken bones back in place, rehab just so she could walk again.

I'm amazed she's doing as well as she is, frankly. I can't blame her if she never wants to put on a pair of skis or a strap her feet to a snowboard again.

It just means my dream of buying that old ski lodge wasn't what was meant for me, I guess. There's no way I'm ever letting go of Pepper. Now that I have her, I can't imagine life without her. And I don't want to.

Hell, she could be pregnant already. That box of condoms from the other day is still in the nightstand drawer, unopened. Things were moving too fast last night. I've never felt like that before, never lost control like that. Heaven knows I put so much cum inside her in that one shot that it's likely to take a month before it all comes back out. And I plan on putting a lot more inside her too.

Just thinking about filling her up with my seed has my dick waking up. If she's not pregnant now, I plan on doing my best to change that. I'd have had her again this morning if I wasn't worried she's too sore.

I watch her add creamer to her coffee and the way she stirs it thoughtfully much longer than needed. I know she's thinking about my questions. Probably wondering how to tell me that the idea of running a ski lodge is about the exact opposite of what she wants to do now.

"It's not that I didn't like it so much," she finally answers after a sip from the steaming mug in her hands. "Once I knew I was never going to get back to the level I was at before, I lost interest. Being out there just doesn't hold any purpose for me anymore."

I'm about to pull her into my arms and tell her how brave she is and how fucking strong she has to be and how much I love her when the squawk-box goes off on the counter where I leave it when I'm home.

The static-y call signal makes both of us jump.

"What is that?" Pepper asks, watching me sprint across the kitchen to grab it off the charger.

"Emergency call," I hastily explain, "I have to check in and see what's up."

Pepper follows, paying close attention to as she listens in on the call I put into my buddy, Erik, the sheriff's deputy for Moonshine Ridge.

"There's a couple of hikers stuck up on the trail

near Mt. Randall," I fill her in when I get off the phone.

I'm already making a sweep of the house, throwing on appropriate clothing and grabbing gear, making a mental check list of what's already in the truck and what I need to grab from the garage.

"So now what?"

"Now you get to hang out in a warm, cozy cabin and snoop through my stuff looking for dark secrets while I grab the skis and the sled and go up and get them down safely."

I grab my keys and phone and pause to kiss the soft lips that are currently pressed together in a thoughtful pout as she watches me prepare to leave.

"Do you have any gear that'll fit me?"

Pepper sets her coffee mug in the sink and heads for the closet she just watched me pull gear from.

"Pep, you don't have to come with me, you can stay here. It's not too serious."

"Yet," she says, firmly, pulling some of my older snow clothes out of the closet.

She heard me talking with Erik. It's not a matter of search and rescue efforts yet. It's just a couple of experienced backpackers in their fifties. They have a communication device and plenty of food, but their gear isn't adequate for the low temps and they knew better than to try to find their way back with the trail under eighteen inches of fresh snow.

All I have to do is ski up with the sled and lead

them down. It's an easy trip, but Pepper knows I'm the only one that's answered the call so far. And she's right, going out alone is never the best plan.

If the tables were turned, nothing would be able to stop me from tagging along if Pepper headed out on her own.

On our way out, I grab skis and boots from the garage for both of us.

"You can wait in the truck with the heater on and the radio," I tell her when I pull to a stop at the trailhead parking forty minutes later.

"Bullshit," she mutters, jumping out and gearing up, "would you stay in the truck while I went?"

"Fuck no."

Chapter Seven

Pepper

It's only a couple of miles off cross-country in the fresh snow but my legs are burning. Of course, it doesn't help that I'm not exactly in the peak athletic shape I was until a few years ago or that my body is still singing from last night's love making.

Still, the muscle memory is still there, propelling me along the trail that Eddy's blazing for me with his easy lead.

The good news is that our stranded hikers are in good shape and even better spirits when we meet up with them. They're experienced hikers and they knew better than to try to find their way out when the snow obliterated the trail.

Eddy pulls high electrolyte sports drinks from

the pack he strapped to the sled and passes them around. After some introductions and a brief bit of chit-chat, he does a quick check on everyone's physical condition and when we've determined everyone is good, Eddy leads our small group out along the trail that's easy to follow now from our skis.

I fall into a sweep position at the back of the line, making sure our hikers are able to keep up and stay with us.

It's slow going on the way back, but a couple of hours later, Eddy and I are swapping skis for snow boots beside his truck and making arrangements to follow the hikers into town where Dr. Everett has already been called in for an emergency visit at the small clinic she oversees in Moonshine Ridge.

The hikers seem fine and eager to check into a room at the lodge and eat their weight in cheeseburgers, but Eddy explains it's standard procedure to have anyone checked out after a recovery of this sort.

Everyone seems understanding and so I climb up into the passenger side of Eddy's truck and let him drive us all back into town.

I'm feeling exhilarated.

"That was awesome," I bounce in my seat and turn to look at Eddy.

"Thank you, I was worried it might not be great since it was your first time and all."

I bat him on the arm with a loud smack. The

muscles there are pumped from carrying gear and I admit the feel of that bicep bulging under the long sleeve shirt he's wearing momentarily has me forgetting why I was giving him shit.

Oh yeah.

"Not *that*!" I swat at his arm again; this time I'm really just looking for an excuse to touch him though.

Eddy grimaces, his eyes still on the road ahead where the snow has given way to dry pavement as we move down in elevation.

"So, you're saying it wasn't amazing and when I get you home, I need to pull out the stops to wow you properly this time?"

"OK, I'm not saying no to that, but I was I talking about the rescue."

Eddy unleashes that dazzling smile and tuns it my way for a second before returning his attention to the mountain road ahead.

"That was hardly a rescue," he scoffs, "more like a retrieval, at best."

"Maybe, but it felt good, you know? Getting out the gear and going out in the back country to help people out. Is that mostly what you guys do?"

"Mostly stuff like this, yeah."

Eddy pulls the truck up in front of the clinic, which is really just a small office built on to the private residence she and her son occupy in the back.

I wait in the truck while Eddy hops out and introduces the hikers to Dr. Everett. Then I wave through the window as they disappear inside with the doctor.

"Sometimes we get called on more dangerous stuff, but we're just volunteer. We're the ones that get called in for non-emergency stuff. It's mostly winching flat-landers off the four-wheel drive trails, to be honest," he continues when he's back in the driver's seat. "So, you liked it, huh?"

"Well duh, I mean, I'm still a little sore but I'm definitely down to be properly wowed when we get back to your place."

This time it's Eddy that reaches out. He doesn't swat at me like I did him, his hand lands on my thigh and squeezes playfully.

"I may have created a monster," he chides. "I meant the recovery stuff. You liked doing that? Skis and all?'

"Skis and all," I confirm.

Eddy's fingers trace along the inside of my thigh, moving higher as he drives us back to his cabin and I think about today and about Eddy and how crazy it is that things can be so uncertain and then suddenly click into place over night.

Eddy

Retreat to the Mountain

I almost let her suck me off this time.

Once we got inside, Pepper was all over me. We didn't even make it up to the bedroom before she had my pants around my ankles and my thick cock down her throat.

Looking down at her while her hand works around the length of my shaft, following her sweet lips as they suck and slide till I'm on the edge like this has me overcome with the need to get inside her.

Call it instinct, call it primal, I don't fucking know what it is, but I need to come inside her again. I need to pump her sweet little womb full of my seed.

Pulling her off my dick with a wet pop when her lips come free unexpectedly, I fall back on the sofa. Pausing only long enough to get her naked, I slip my hand between her legs and groan.

"Fuck this pussy's wet, baby." I can't help but push my face into her sex and inhale her aroma before my patience gives out on me.

"Here," I command, pulling her down over me so she's straddling me now, "I want you to ride this naked cock."

My hands grip her hips and guide her down onto me, holding her still just as the broad head of my dick is poised at her entrance.

"Pepper," I'm grappling for control, but I need

her to understand, "I want watch you come on my cock and make me explode inside you."

She nods, her eyes hooded with lust as she runs her hands over my chest. "I want that too, Eddy," she says, her voice thick and hoarse.

"I want you pregnant," I tell her, my hand moving to splay widely over her soft stomach, "I want to fill you up again and again until you're growing my baby inside you. I want to marry you, Pepper. Are you ready for all that?"

To answer me, she breaks my hold and slides down, sheathing my hardness with her tight heat.

"Is that your official proposal, Mr. Jones?"

Pepper gives me a naughty little grin as she pulls me all the way deep inside her.

"Is this your official acceptance?"

Damn it's hard to talk when all I want to do is thrust up into her.

"No," she shakes her head and those dark waves shimmy over her shoulders, brushing over her hard, rosy nipples. Then she starts to move. Long, slow strokes that have me seeing stars when she finishes each one with a grind against the root of my dick before sliding back up slowly again. "But this is."

How the fuck can she keep moving so slowly. It feels so fucking good, all I want to do is yank her down hard and rut into her. My arms tighten around her waist, my hips working to drive myself deeper into her with each one of her languid strokes until her rhythm changes and we're both moving frantically.

Pepper's so close. I can see it in her eyes, I can feel the flutter of her walls around me. When I reach between us and press my thumb to her clit, she goes off like a rocket. Her back arches, her cry bounces off the ceiling beams, and her tight channel squeezes down on my rod and pulses till I can't hang on anymore either.

When neither of us have energy left to stay sitting up, we collapse together on the couch.

"I'm on the pill," Pepper whispers, her breath cool against my sweaty chest.

"Well get off it." I drop a kiss on top of her head and fold my arms even more tightly around her. "Why do you need to be on it anyway?"

"It helped with my cycles when I was competing, I just never thought about stopping till now."

"I meant it, Pepper," I say against her forehead when she tips her face up toward me, "as soon as you're ready, married, babies, the whole picket fence plan. I love you. I want to build a life with you."

"We can skip the picket fence." She mumbles, snuggling against me.

"I'll build you whatever kind of fence you want, baby."

Epilogue 1
One Month Later

Pepper

I got my official proposal a few weeks ago, complete with a gorgeous diamond ring and my father's approval.

We're planning our wedding for next summer and today, I have Eddy driving us to check out a potential venue. At least, that's the story I gave him. I have a surprise for Eddy that I've waited long enough to share.

"Right here, turn here," I direct, waving my hand frantically at the turn off before Eddy misses it.

"Babe, this road doesn't go anywhere but the old lodge I was telling you about."

"It doesn't?" I think I'm doing a pretty good job of playing dumb, personally.

"Yeah, see? Right there, that's the old ski lodge."

He points through the windshield at the boarded-up property just ahead.

"Hmm, weird, this is the address I have."

After helping those hikers off the trail last month, I knew I wasn't done being on the snow after all. It's just going to be different for me now. No more fast downhills, jumps, or slaloms in my future. I'll be getting my adrenaline rushes in other ways.

Partly by helping Eddy and the rest of the crew out with the rescue and recovery jobs when I can, partly by helping my future husband realize his dream.

"Well, just pull up to the front and park," I say, "I guess while we're here we might as well look around."

Eddy's been excited that I'm interested in doing some skiing, and maybe a bit of snowboarding, again but I know he didn't expect me to be interested in reopening the old lodge.

I couldn't stand the thought of him giving up on his dream because of me. That's not my idea of a partnership. I think a good partnership finds ways to make dreams come true that benefits both of us.

Eddy parks the truck and we get out. He's busy telling me all about the place, memories he has of working the winter seasons for the original owners, visions he had for what he wanted to do with it.

He's been rattling on so enthusiastically; it took

him this long to realize the door is open and I'm inside.

"The door was unlocked?" He's confused and sounds a little irritated at the thought that some irresponsible real estate agent might have left the place unsecured.

I hold up the key chain with the little snowman dangling off it. "The door was locked," I assure him.

"You have the key?"

Finally. *Finally,* understanding starts to dawn in Eddy's eyes as pieces start to fall together.

That bright grin flashes at me as he walks across the lobby to join me by the giant fireplace built from stone quarried up at the river. I got the whole history on the place when I put in my initial inquiry.

"Pepper, what's going on?"

I try to keep a straight face but I just can't contain my excitement, not when I see the hopefulness shadowing his blue eyes.

"The contractor said it'll take at least six months to get the place operational," I mention casually. "And that isn't including the lift, which requires a whole different type of contractor and some permits to update it to meet current codes. I figure we have a lot of work to do if we want to be open for next year's season."

"What are you telling me, baby?"

He knows my financial situation is pretty solid

from smart investments made with my endorsement income back when I was a top snowboarder. Now I fill him in on the deal I've been working on to buy the old ski lodge out of foreclosure and get it up and running again.

"No," Eddy tells me firmly, "I don't want you risking all your money on a project that could still go belly up. I want you to keep that money invested for the future."

"This is our future, Eddy," I explain, "and I'm not risking everything. I have a couple of investors going in with me. My old coach in interested in using Moonshine Ridge as her training ground. That will be a huge return right off the bat. We can do this. If you want to?"

Eddy's eyes light up and he swoops me off my feet to twirl me around the expansive, empty room. Then he plants his lips on mine in a kiss that has me thinking this drafty old lodge needs a proper christening, and I know exactly what his answer is going to be when we come up for air.

Epilogue 2
One Year Later

Eddy

"So, you think it'll get here in time, then?"

"It's a big order. We might have to hire a freight company to get it all up here in one trip, but we should be able to arrange delivery in plenty of time."

Ash and I hash out the logistics of getting the orders Pepper and I need in time for our opening.

The lodge still needs a lot of work, but we'll be able to run partially open as soon as we get a good enough storm for the snow to stick.

Pep and I moved into the on-site living quarters at the lodge as soon as we had them renovated. It just makes more sense for us to be living up there since we're the ones who will be providing most of the labor for running the place.

And, since Pepper found out she's pregnant, there was no way we were going to be able to stay in my one-bedroom A-frame much longer anyway. The apartment at the lodge is a three bed/two bath. Perfect for a growing family.

Hyacinth and Ash just found out they're expecting again too, so the girls have been inseparable lately with a ton a mommy-to-be talk that's over my head. I'm just glad Pepper has a good friend to walk her through her first baby jitters. Turns out, I'm pretty damn glad I have a buddy to walk me through mine too.

"How you holdin' up there?" Ash shoots a glance at the back room where our wives are busy talking girl talk.

"Which part?" I laugh. "The puking? The mood swings? Or the demanding sex life?"

"Oh damn, you got all of it all at once, huh?"

Ash laughs again and this time I laugh with him.

Yeah, Pepper's first trimester was a roller coaster ride for sure. She just hit four months and we exchanged one set of symptoms for new ones. Now it's cravings, and naps, and demands for my cock.

"Can't complain though," I tell him, "I've never been happier."

"I know what you mean, man," Ash agrees, nodding sagely as we go back to figuring out how to get the rental skis and boards to the lodge in time for opening.

"Hey," Pepper says as she and Hyacinth re-join us out front, "we're headed down to the tavern to grab some burgers, you guys coming?"

"Don't let Alice see you," Ash warns Pepper, "she still comes over here at least once a week to bitch about how you abandoned her."

"Jeesh," Pepper scoffs, rolling her eyes, "I gave her like, six months, notice. It's not like she even wanted me there anyway."

"Yeah, well that old lady can hold a grudge like no one I've ever known," Hyacinth points out.

Ash hangs the "back in an hour" sign in the window and locks the door as we head out.

The tavern's just a short walk down the street from Ash's sporting goods store and the four of us are walking two by two on the sidewalk, Ash and I both have our arms wrapped protectively around our women, making small talk as we go.

The weather is mild for early November but there's a nip in the air warning that winter's about to hit hard.

"Who's that?" Pepper asks, raising her hand to wave a woman across the street.

"Never seen her before" I answer, lifting my hand to return the woman's wave.

"Looks like she rented number eight over there," Ash muses as our whole party's attention turns to the curvy blonde pulling the "for rent" sign out of the window of the storefront marked with a numeral eight above the door.

"Wonder what she's going to do?" I pose the question to no one in particular as I hold the door of the tavern open for the others to file through.

Shooting a glance back over my shoulder to the empty windows across the street where the stranger can barely be seen standing in the middle of the vacant suite, I wonder if she has any clue what she's getting herself into.

Driven to the Mountain

About

Current Jones

It's the biggest news on the ridge since Birch McAllister cleared his family name: one of the shops downtown got rented.

Moonshine Ridge is a tight community. We like to think we're welcoming, but opening a new business in a town where no one knows you? That's a recipe for failure in a place that tends to support its own.

The truth is, you'd be best to establish some local connections that can vouch for you if you want to be successful up on the ridge.

So, when I get my first look at the woman standing on a ladder with a paint roller in her hand, I tell myself my intentions are purely neighborly; that the soft curves and determined spirit that have me out of my mind with need have nothing to do with spending all my time helping her to get her brewery up and running.

I'm going to make sure Ginger's new business is a success here on the ridge and then I'm going to claim her soft body and make her mine, because I knew the moment I laid eyes on her that the real reason Ginger was driven to the mountain was to be my wife.

Welcome to Moonshine Ridge and the rugged wilderness surrounding the remote mountain community where the history is long, the local lore is deep, and the men are as wild as the mountains they come from.

Protective, possessive, totally obsessed; the men of Moonshine Ridge will do anything necessary to claim the women they love and give her the happily ever after she deserves.

The Moonshine Ridge books contain a lot of insta-love, some swearing, some steamy scenes, zero cheating, and a lot of swoon-worthy happy endings. They're interconnected with recurring characters but can be read as stand-alones in any order.

Copyright © 2023 Rocklyn Ryder

All rights reserved worldwide
No part of this book may be reproduced, uploaded to the Internet, or copied without permission from the author. The author respectfully asks that you please support artistic expression and help promote anti-piracy efforts by purchasing a copy of this book at the authorized online outlets.

This is a work of fiction intended for mature audiences only. Names, characters, places, and incidents either are the product of the author's imagination or are used fictitiously. Any resemblance to events, locales, business establishments, or actual persons, living or dead, events, or locales is purely coincidental.

Chapter One

Ginger

It's not what I had in mind, but I can work with it...the original plan was to open the brewery in my hometown, down in Slow River. After jumping through hoops with City Hall for almost an entire year, they finally put their official rubber stamp on the stack of paperwork that represented all my hopes and dreams.

It said "denied."

My patience, and my budget, are a lot lower than when I first decided to take my home brewing hobby to the next level-- opening up my own microbrewery and tap house.

I was about to give up when my friend suggested thinking outside the box-- the box on the map that represents the borders of Slow River where the rents are high and the permit process is apparently impossible.

Moonshine Ridge is a two-hour drive from the valley. It's a small town. Like, Slow River is what most people think of when you say "small town;" Moonshine Ridge is itty bitty.

But it had available space with ridiculously cheap rent, and although the county licensing is still the same, the permits that Slow River refused to issue me are non-existent up here.

Mrs. Hart literally took my check for my deposit and first month's rent, handed me the keys, and said "you're not gonna blow the place up, right?"

With a lot of hustle, and the rest of my savings, I should be opening to serve my first batch of brew to the good people of Moonshine Ridge sometime next spring.

Looking out the window, I take in the view of the locals that are out and about in the warm weather of this early fall day.

A woman waves shyly at me from across the street. She's walking with a man who has his arm wrapped around her shoulder in a way that shouts "mine." When she waves, the bearded man turns and scowls in my direction, along with the other couple that's walking with them.

They're headed for the tavern and I get the feeling they may not be happy to see a stranger opening up a brewery across the street.

Moonshine Ridge is definitely not the hipster scene from downtown Slow River; I have a feeling the gruff and rugged mountain men up here would rather sit in a dank bar shooting pool and tossing peanut shells on the floor while they swill mass produced American lagers from tall-boy mugs.

That's fine. I'm not relying on local traffic to keep me afloat. I've got bigger ideas than that.

Current

Everyone on the ridge is talking about it, the space in town that just rented out. To an outsider, no less.

The news reached me all the way up here at Riverbend, where most of my family has lived for the last hundred and fifty years since my great, great blah blah grandfather originally staked his mining claim right along the river's shoreline.

We're about fifteen miles up the mountain from the edge of what most people would consider anything resembling "town," and once the rafting season ends in early September, the only way we get news up here is-- well. My grandmother, mostly.

Grandma V is what happens when the hippies

from the sixties don't outgrow being hippies. She's about eight-one or two now and going strong. Still has feathers in her hair, still wears long flowing skirts that she sews from scrap fabric so she looks like a walking crazy quilt with her waist length silver hair blowing in the wind.

Grandma V is the best.

I count myself lucky as hell that me and my brothers got to grow up right here on our family's land, spending our days with Vera and Don. Getting raised on fresh food that came from our own homestead garden-- the goats really only showed up a few years ago, but that's a whole 'nother story.

Vera happens to be close friends with Mable Hart, however. Mable runs the local museum in town which also serves as the closest thing Moonshine Ridge has to a visitor's center; and she owns the row of commercial real estate that her own great grandfather built back in the 1870s.

Most of the suites have been empty for years. Sometimes someone here in town gets a grand scheme to open a knitting shop or a scrapbooking store. Once, Howard Smalls got it in his head that the ridge needed a hookah bar. That lasted about two weeks.

It took that long for Howard to pack his hookah pipes up and move out.

So when some a flat-lander shows up in Moonshine Ridge to rent the largest space in the row,

Mable couldn't wait to come up here and fill in Grandma V and the rest of us Joneses.

Apparently, it's just one woman and she's opening a brewery.

If you ask me, that's going to go over about as well as Howard's hookah lounge. The ridge isn't much for the fancy craft brew scene that's taken over downtown Slow River, and the locals are likely to stay loyal to their own. And that's Cedar McAllister's tavern.

Then my brother, Eddy, and his wife were up for dinner at the house a few days ago and asked if I'd been to town to check out the progress on the new business yet. Said it's not looking good for her if she's planning on opening anytime soon.

I guess I finally got sick of being the last one to know what the biggest news in town is since the McAllisters managed to clear their family name.

That's how I found myself in town, standing in the empty space marked with a simple number eight over the door. A curvy blonde with a paint roller dripping gray paint onto her face is singing along with a Bob Marley tune that must be playing through her earbuds, and all I can think is that the barefoot woman in the tie-dyed pants is going to be mine.

Chapter Two

Ginger

Another glob of dark gray paint drips off the roller and lands on my boobs. If there's a better way to pain a ceiling, I'd like to know what it is. I mean, outside of hiring a professional. Which I can't afford at this point.

Besides, I like the idea of doing it myself. This way, the business gets imbued with my passion and vision for what I want it to become.

Keeping those positive vibes in mind, I keep coating the bland, acoustic ceiling tiles with the "stormy day" gray paint and sing along with Bob as he convinces me it's going to be all right.

It's one of the more obvious additions on my "Don't Panic" playlist and it does the trick, keeping me from wallowing in the negative thoughts about how much harder this has been than I'd expected and worries of whether or not I'll be successful up here in this tiny mountain town where no one knows me.

With a stretch, I use the extension handle on the roller to reach all the way to the edges where I spent all day yesterday carefully taping off the walls. The ladder wobbles under my bare feet, but doesn't tip. I use my toes to grab on to the upper rung, the one right above the one that says I shouldn't stand any higher, of course. But it's a high ceiling and the five-foot step-ladder was the only one in my parents' garage so it's what I have to work with.

More paint flies off the roller and splatters over me as the roller works its way back toward me from the corner.

This time, there's enough paint that's landed on my face that I'm going to need to climb down the ladder and wash it off.

"Ohmygod!" The paint roller clangs on the unfinished concrete floor, sending paint flying in all directions for a ten-foot radius.

"You scared me," I tell the man standing only a few feet from my ladder.

Quickly pulling the ear buds out of my ears, I scramble down the ladder-- which he quickly reaches out and takes hold of to steady it for me.

"Sorry." The tall, blonde, bearded, Viking *god* says with a smile that was made for melting panties.

"I didn't mean to scare you, I just wanted to come down and see what all the fuss is about."

"What fuss?" I ask, picking up the dropped roller and grabbing some rags to try to clean up some of the splattered paint.

Before I can manage to smear paint over the concrete, however, this guy has grabbed a couple of the rags from my pile, run them under the faucet in the bathroom, and is back; carefully wiping up the worst of the spills without leaving the blurred, gray mess behind that I'm doing such a great job of.

"You're hired," I tease, pointing at his far superior painting clean up skills.

He laughs; one of those short, under-his-breath, chuckles like I made him feel self-conscious or something.

"Hey, I'm Ginger." I choose this perfectly awkward pause between us to announce my name, shoving my hand toward him for a paint-stained shake.

"Current." He stands up to his full height, which I'm estimating to be somewhere in the neighborhood of don't-hit-your-head-on-my-twelve-foot-ceiling, and takes my hand to shake it.

His touch feels like sinking into a hot bath at the end of a hard day. His huge hand engulfs mine in a warm and callused caress.

"Like the events? Or the fruit?" I'm trying to picture his name in my mind.

"Like the flow of a river."

A flash of that smile has me all too aware of the current running through my body right now. First, the electrical one emanating from where our hands are still joined, and then, the gush of fluid spreading between my legs.

"Sorry," I stammer, taking my hand back reluctantly and forcing myself back to reality. "You said there was a fuss about something?"

Current

Just...*wow*. This girl has me tied in knots.

From the moment I peered around the edge of the open door and got my first look at her, I've been fighting the urge to throw her over my shoulder, caveman style. Or throw her down, or up against a wall, or just see what kind of damage we could do to this ladder.

She's more than sexy as hell though; all five foot nothing of her and curvy as fuck with that long, straight, hair pulled back in a simple pony tail hanging loosely down her back.

Her hair's a sandy sort of strawberry blonde; the amber hue of sun-dried wheat, and the eyes that are staring back at me with all the same intensity are a shade of gray like the smoky quartz crystals I sometimes find up by the hot springs.

She's wearing almost as much of the paint as she got on the ceiling tiles. There's a fine spray across her forehead, nose, and cheeks like a mist of dark gray freckles, and thick smear running from just below one eye to her jawline. It's in her hair, it's on her neck, and it's especially concentrated in large dots that have soaked through the cropped, black, t-shirt over her generous breasts.

The tie-dye pants are cut wide like pajamas and when I drop my eyes to complete the full picture-- because I'm going to be using it later when I'm alone, for sure-- I see there's even a splotch of dried paint on the top of one of her bare feet, along with the turquoise, glitter nail polish and a silver toe-ring that wraps around the second toe of her left foot.

There's something about Ginger that has me thinking about more than all the ways I'm aching to explore her body. She feels like home.

"Yeah, you're the most exciting thing that's happened on the ridge in the last few years," I finally answer her when she takes her hand from mine.

Instinctively I start to reach to take it back when I remember we just met. My heart has us married with a bunch of wild kids running all over the mountain already, and it takes more than a little self-control to keep my manners.

"What did I do?" Ginger gives me a genuinely perplexed look and then starts gathering paint supplies.

I follow her to the big utility sink in the far back of the empty space and help her rinse out rags and paint rollers.

"You rented a pad in town...and no one knows who you are."

She uses one of the wet rags to scrub at the paint that's dried on her arms. When she gets to her face, I stop her and take the rag from her hand.

Ginger stands statue still for me while I lightly scrub the paint splatters from her face. Her eyes are closed and her face is turned up toward me.

Ginger's head tips back a little farther, her lips stay parted slightly as I get the last bit of paint to come off from where it was smudged into the fine hairs in front of her ear.

She has three tiny, silver hoops lining that ear, but only one in the other ear.

My thumb grazes lightly along the little hollow where the paint was a few seconds ago. My head lowers, turning one side as I close the space with every intention of kissing her.

Chapter Three

Ginger

"Hello?"

Female voices call hesitantly from somewhere just outside the door that's still standing wide open, propped by one of the buckets of paint.

Current's hands are off me and I can feel the lack of his presence even before I open my eyes again. He's suddenly a good six feet away from me, busying himself with wringing out the wet rags we just rinsed.

"Hello? Is anyone here?" The voices are on this side of the open door now and I move out from behind the dividing wall that separates the utility room and bathrooms from main area.

"Yes? Can I help you?" I ask, seeing the trio of

women stepping over drop cloths and painting supplies.

One of them is clearly pregnant and the blonde has a box in her arms filled with what appear to be take-out containers from a restaurant.

"Hi, I'm Hyacinth." The redhead makes a beeline for me with her hand outstretched. "This is Cami," she says, indicating the blonde, "and Terra."

Terra waves at me from across the room and reaches to take the box from Cami, who immediately braces her hand against the side of her baby bump.

"She just started kicking," she explains, smiling even while wincing, "and she's good at it."

"Wait a few months," Hyacinth tells her friend, "It's only going to get worse."

"Do you have a table?" Terra lifts up the boxes of boxes.

"Hang on, I might have something in the truck."

Current emerges from behind the wall and I watch my visitors all stare at him as he darts out the door to a lifted four by four parked just outside.

"Looks like Current beat us to welcoming you to town." Hyacinth peers through the big, front window and watches as Current pulls some things from the bed of his truck.

"How are you liking Moonshine Ridge so far?" Cami asks.

Current returns with a couple of camp chairs,

which he quickly sets up and Cami grabs one immediately.

"Um, I don't really know," I answer Cami's last question absently while I watch Current jog to the sporting goods store across the street. "I haven't really met anybody in town yet."

"Well, you've met Current Jones," Terra says, "and you had to have met Mable Hart, since she owns this building, and now you've met us." She says it triumphantly as she sets the box down on the small folding table that Current just returned with and starts pulling out the smaller boxes as Current sets up a few more camp chairs that he also brought from across the street.

"My husband, Cedar, and I own the tavern across the street," Cami is saying. "You haven't been in at all so we figured you might not have eaten anything yet."

The take-out boxes are full of burgers and chili-cheese fries and fried pickle spears. A bottle of soda and some cups appear from the bag that Hyacinth was carrying.

Everyone is talking and I'm trying to keep up with all the information that's getting dropped on me so suddenly.

I appreciate the welcoming committee; Hyacinth apologizes for taking a few days to come over.

"Mable told Vera who told Marcia that you weren't interested in being bothered so we kinda held back but then it seemed like you were doing a bunch of work all by yourself and then Alice said she hadn't even met you yet which meant you hadn't been to the store at all because we all know Alice is not coming over here to introduce herself."

I dig a thick, home-cut fry into chili that is obviously not from a can, dizzy from trying to follow all the voices and the names they are dropping.

With a look up at Current, I shrug.

He gives me one of those winning smiles I like so much, and grabs the big, five-gallon bucket for mixing the paint for the walls, flips it over and sits down right next to me so he can steal my fries.

The girls keep talking and I keep trying to follow along, but I'm too aware of Current beside me.

Warmth radiates off his body and he's close enough that I can smell the masculine scent of him; a combination of spice and fresh cut timber that suits the mountains around us.

"So what are you going to do in here, anyway?" Terra finally breaks through the gibberish of names and places that I'm not familiar with to ask me something I know the answer to.

"I brew beer," I say, proudly. "I'm opening a craft brewery with a tap house. Six to eight of my own brews in rotation and four guest taps."

Current

I can see the pride on her face, hear it in her voice. My girl believes in her plan.

Ginger goes on excitedly, explaining that she started home brewing as a science experiment when she was taking classes down at the Slow River community college.

She really got into the process, and started experimenting with different recipes and styles. Two years ago, she won a state competition for her porter, which she wants to showcase as her house brew.

The more she talks, the more excited I get for her plan. Not because Moonshine Ridge needs another place to grab a beer after work, but because it's so obviously her passion.

The other women in the room, however, are staring at her like she's speaking a foreign language.

"So you're going to make beer." Terra sums it up pretty succinctly and I have to snag another chili and cheese drenched fry from the box in Ginger's hands to stifle my amusement.

Terra is the baby of the Diaz brood at eighteen. I've known her since she was born. She's a little spitfire with a take no prisoners attitude. With three hulking brothers, the Diaz girls grew up tough.

"Yeah, that's the plan," Ginger gives the girl a

patient smile and fights me for the last fry in the box.

"But why Moonshine Ridge?" Cami asks. "Why not open your brewery in Slow River? It's bigger, it's already got a craft beer scene. Don't you think you'd do better down there?"

"That was my plan," Ginger says, "but City Hall denied my permits. I lost money on a place I'd already rented and now I'm paying to store the equipment I'd already ordered in anticipation of opening down there. A friend of mine finally suggested up here because there's no city permitting required for what I want to do. Just the business license with the county. And rent is a lot cheaper."

"I hate to say it. I mean, Cami and I are both pretty new to the ridge too, but--"

"But no one in Moonshine Ridge knows you," Terra interjects. "This is a tight community, and you're coming in as competition to the only bar in town. You're not connected to anyone on the ridge and--"

Cami and Hyacinth exchange a glance and I know what they're thinking. It's the same thing that's been bothering me since I walked in and realized that no matter what Ginger wanted to do here, I wanted her to succeed.

"People on the ridge tend to support their own," Terra says.

Ginger swallows hard and forces a smile as she nods in understanding.

"Yeah, I worry about that. But as long as we're not talking about all out sabotage or anything, I don't need the tap house to be successful. I'll be making most of my profits from bottling and distributing small batches to retailers."

"That's smart," I butt in. "But do you have retailers lined up already? Or is that just your big picture plan?"

Ginger turns those gray eyes on me and the other three women in the room fade into the walls behind them. Damn, this woman is already everything for me.

"I have contracts with four places right now, that should be enough to keep me in business if I can just afford the expenses until I can fill orders. I still have to get my state alcohol licensing clear."

Hyacinth's phone buzzes and she tells us that Ash is ready to close up the store and could she and Terra please come back and take over baby-sitting duties of their one-year-old daughter, Rose.

"On it!" Terra jumps up and gives Ginger a quick hug. "Welcome to the Ridge, Ginger," she says as she heads for the doorway. "I can't drink yet but I'll tell my brothers to be nice to you and not give you shit about making fancy beer."

Ginger laughs and waves after the young girl

who's running across the street to rescue Hyacinth's husband from his own first born.

Hyacinth helps Cami to her feet and they take turns giving Ginger quick hugs as well.

"We thought she could use a little extra money from the babysitting job," Hyacinth explains as she gestures toward Terra's escape route. "Now she calls herself the nanny and we barely get to hold our own daughter."

Ginger and I stand and Hyacinth shakes her head and waves me off when I offer to carry things back to the store.

"We can pick them up tomorrow," Hy says. "We're right across the street, we'll be seeing plenty of each other."

Cami and Hyacinth tell us both goodbye and head back the way they came, no doubt bursting to share all the news that just learned.

"I think I'm done here for the day," Ginger says, looking around at the space that still has a long way to go before she'll be anywhere near ready to start business.

"I'd invite you up for dinner but--" I wave toward the empty boxes left from the burgers and fries we just gorged ourselves on. "If you want, you could come up and watch a movie. I'd love to hear more about your business plan."

"I'd love to."

The way her pupils dilate when she looks up and

me, and her voice goes airy, I think she means it. The anticipation has my dick swelling already.

"But I can't. It's a two-hour drive back down to the valley and I have to start my application for the alcohol licenses tomorrow."

"When are you going to be back?" I gather up the trash, trying to keep busy so I don't give in to that inner caveman that's still desperate to throw her over my shoulder.

"Day after tomorrow. I still have so much work to get done."

"I'll meet you here. Eight A.M. too early?"

Her eyes bug and she laughs, "Yes. Way. But I'm willing to compromise if it means you'll be here. Make it ten."

"Ten." I have an arm full of trash to take out to the dumpster. That makes going in for a proper kiss awkward as fuck. I wait while she locks up and then settle for landing a peck on her cheek before she gets in her car to leave.

"Thanks, Current," she calls out from the open window, "I'm looking forward to seeing you soon."

Watching as she pulls out and disappears out of sight around the bend in the road on her way out of town, I sigh heavily and head for the bear-proof corral where the dumpster for the building is.

The next thirty-six hours are going to be tough.

Chapter Four

Ginger

After a long day of phone calls and spending hours listening to horrible music on hold while getting transferred to about a hundred different departments with the state's alcoholic beverage licensing division, I'm ready for a drink of my own.

"Please tell me you can meet me at O'Hare's," I beg my friend, Callie.

"I don't get off work till seven," she tells me, adding a sprig of baby's breath into the arrangement she's working on.

"The shop closes at six, though," I point out.

Callie laughs at my impatience and sets the new bouquet in the big fridge before washing her hands.

"Yeah, but there's a ton of clean up to do after

locking up. I have to count out the till and double check that all the deliveries scheduled for tomorrow are ready to go.

"You're going to be finding out for yourself just how much work there is to do after work." She dries her hands and points at me. "Speaking of your impending self-employment, how's it going? Are you still on schedule to be open by April?"

A glance at the clock on the wall behind Callie's head tells me it's just six now. Callie locks the front door and flips the hand-painted sign in the window to the side that reads "closed."

We have another hour or so before she'll be ready to leave.

Dropping my head to the counter surface I let out a loud groan to answer her question.

"That good, huh?" she laughs, then pats my head before getting to work on cleaning things up and making sure everything is ready to go for her manager when she opens in the morning.

Callie and I have been friends since grade school. She's a couple years younger than me, at twenty-two, but we lived only two houses apart when we were little. Slow River is definitely old school in the way that you grow up playing with the kids you live nearest to.

Parents weren't packing up the kids and hauling them to fancy recreation centers or community parks for organized play dates when I was growing up.

Cal and I were playing in the irrigation ditch by the corn fields, catching tadpoles with our bare hands every summer right up until one of us discovered boys.

I'm ashamed to say, that was Callie.

She was definitely the girlier one of us and I still remember the summer she first laid eyes on Dean O'Leary. He was nothing but a scrawny farm boy back then, all of nineteen but all my nine-year-old bestie saw was hearts and happily ever after.

He told us that girls that played in the mud were gross and I don't think Cal's made a mud pie since.

That was over a decade ago.

Dean's still single, so Callie's still crushing.

"I'm ready," Callie declares, grabbing her stuff and waiting for me to catch up with her as she holds the back door open and sets the alarm. "Walk and talk, girl. I want a full report on your opening plans and then I want to hear about all the bearded hotties up on the ridge."

By the time we have a seat in the back room of O'Hare's Saloon and our first round of their house special Kentucky Mules-- a standard Moscow Mule made with bourbon instead of vodka-- I've given Callie the full update on my day's saga with the alcohol licensing board.

"I can't believe how difficult it is just to figure

out which licenses I even need," I tell her as I point at the sampler platter on the happy hour menu for our waitress. "It's like they don't even know. I kept getting transferred from one department to another. I think I spent more on hold than actually talking to people today. If I hear one more instrumental version of Fleetwood Mac, you'll need bail money."

One empty, copper mug gets exchanged for a full one and I'm thinking it's a good thing I walked down town tonight. Slow River has exactly one taxi and two ride share drivers-- all of whom are notoriously unavailable after eight p.m. on weeknights.

Luckily, Main Street is an easy walk from my place.

"Dang, who's pouring tonight? These things are strong!"

Maybe I just sucked the first one down too fast, but my head is spinning already and I'm usually good for two of these before I feel it.

Callie cranes her neck to get a look into the main bar. "Emilio," she reports.

"If he keeps pouring heavy like this, Virgie's likely to kick him back down to bar back." I can't help but laugh. It's probably the booze, but I'm suddenly feeling a lot less stressed out.

Virginia Stockebrand is the current owner of O'Hare's. She's in her mid-seventies, built like a Viking warrior, takes no shit, and gives no fucks. If Emilio keeps pouring heavy like this, he'd better be saving his tip money, because Virgie will take her lost revenue out of his hide.

"OK, so you got through all the applications though?" Callie asks, as we dig into the nachos. "Now what?"

"I met a guy."

Oops. Not sure I was planning on telling her about Current. At least, not just yet. The mention of him has me going flushed and that's not the alcohol. I get hot all over every time I think of him, and I've spent a lot of time thinking about him since we parted ways yesterday.

"Oh Em Gee!" Callie's eyes are wide as she stares at me like she's never seen me before. "Are those hearts I see in my best friend's eyes? *Finally?*"

Callie giggles like we're teenagers again and raises a hand to signal to our waitress that we need another round. Which I probably don't, but I know Callie is about to launch into full interrogation mode.

I've never really fallen in love before and she knows it. I've crushed hard a few times but it's never lasted very long. Unlike Cal, I've done some of experimenting with boys.

If she's seeing hearts in my eyes right now-- it's not the booze.

"Don't order the wedding flowers yet," I caution. "I just met him yesterday. I didn't even get his number."

"But you're going to see him again?"

Fighting what I know is a goofy grin, I nod. "He's meeting me tomorrow to help with the painting."

"You're letting a man help you with the place? Someone call the Times, Ginger's in love!"

"Shh!" I shush her hard and fast, "Don't jinx it."

"Ginge, are you serious? You don't think he's just another crush?"

I give her a weak shrug and stir the melting ice in my mug with my straw. "This feels different somehow," I admit. "This guy's special."

Current

Eighteen more hours to go till I see Ginger again. Not that I'm counting or anything.

"Hey Mom," I bend down and give her a peck on the cheek, snaking my hand around the side of her to snatch a fresh cookie off the cooling rack. "Where are V and Don?"

Mom rolls her eyes as she plays dumb to my cookie thievery without an admonishment about spoiling my dinner.

"Vera's out in the garden, I think she's digging carrots for supper. Don's at the dock with Eddy and Pepper and I think River's down there with them."

"Dad and Rapid?"

"Rapid isn't back from town yet, I think he said he needed to stop by the clinic for a refill on a prescription."

"Sure seems like Rapid's been sick a lot lately."

Mom drops her eyes back the tray she just pulled out of the oven and chuckles to herself. "Yeah, he's some kind of sick, all right," she mutters so low I barely hear.

"Get your dad in here so he can get the meat on the grill, would you? Some of us would prefer to eat before midnight."

"Got it." I grin, steal another one of the chocolate chip cookies off the rack, and head out the back door to search for my dad.

The Joneses don't get together regularly for big family dinners. I guess we figure that between living up here on the same land and working together all summer with the rafting outfit, we see plenty enough of each other throughout the week.

But Eddy got married last year and he and Pepper are expecting their first baby soon. That, and the fact that they bought the old ski lodge a few miles up the mountain and have been working overtime to get it ready to open this season; I guess Mom's been feeling like she needs to get us together more often.

She does that by bribing us with red meat and fresh baked goods. A few weeks ago, it was fresh huckleberry cobbler; I think every one of us showed early for that one.

After I get dad wrangled back to help Mom out, I find Grandma V on her way back from the garden with an armful of fresh-dug carrots in a rainbow of colors. Don likes to tease her that she doesn't like vegetables that are the "right" color. The carrots are white and purple and yellow. She also grows tomatoes that are green when ripe and claims the orange watermelons are sweeter than traditional red ones.

Years ago, I remember she was excited about finding a variety of bell peppers that turned purple and the first time she threw some in an omelet they lost the purple color and turned ordinary green...she's still mad that the "purple was a lie."

"Need help with those?" I ask as I take the bundles of muddy carrots from her without waiting for her answer.

"Don't you go eating those, now," Vera tells me sternly, "I intentionally didn't wash them off because I knew if I did, you'd have 'em gone before we get back to the house."

"No worries, Grandma V," I promise with a laugh-- she knows me too well. "I already spoiled my appetite with cookies."

Of all of us boys, I'm the only one that calls Vera "grandma" and even though her and Don raised their kids and all of us grand-kids to call them by their first names-- something about wanting us to know that we're all equals in the family-- it never felt right to me.

Secretly, I think this makes me Grandma's favorite.

The family is starting to wander back to the patio outside Mom's country style kitchen with the "ceremonial lighting of the Q--" a term coined by grandpa Don back when Dad got his first gas grill and promptly spent an hour trying to light it.

Drove him crazy that he could light a campfire and man a camp stove, but the big grill eluded him. Now it's a bit of a tradition for us to gather around while he lights it even though he's an old pro at pushing that button these days.

Grandma emerges from the house with an armful of cold beers and hands one to me, one to Don, and pops the last one for herself. Then she pulls a freshly washed carrot from her apron pocket and slips it to me on the sly like we're passing notes in class.

It's a yellow one.

The sound of an older diesel engine sputtering to a stop in the drive out front signals my oldest brother's arrival.

Gopher, the border collie mix that's been the collective pet of the family since he showed up on the property as a half-drowned pup a few years back, rushes to great him and a minute later, Rapid appears around the corner with a beer already in his hand, and a shit-eating grin on his face while he whistles some upbeat tune.

Something is definitely up with my big brother. He's always been the grump of the family, this whistling habit he's picked up is starting to creep me out.

"Hey little brothers," Rapid greets the rest of us, landing a loud slap on my shoulder. "Peps," he nods at Pepper, "how's everybody doing?"

He commandeers the half-eaten carrot from my hand and says thanks like I offered it to him, same as he's been doing to me since we were kids.

A round of answers comes his way and we all nod and reply appropriately, acknowledging Pepper's due date, Mom's plea to not eat all the cookies before dinner, and Dad's insistence that the tri-tips will be done in "twenty minutes" even though we all know better.

When eyes turn my way, I take a drink from the can of light beer in my hand and I swear I can't stop the grin on my face when I fill my family in on my own update: "I met the girl I'm going to marry."

Chapter Five

Ginger

Current is already waiting for me when I pull up in front of the building, but then again, I am seventeen minutes late.

"Sorry." I rush through my apologies as I hurry to unlock the door, "I'm not really a morning person...and there might have been one too many mules last night. Please tell me you haven't been waiting long."

Current waits patiently while I talk a mile a minute and then flashes that panty-melting grin. Is ten in the morning too early to start day-dreaming about this guy? I hope not. Because I started day-dreaming at seven while I was in the shower.

"Mules?" He asks.

"Uh, yeah, one of the bars in town makes these drinks--"

"Moscow mules?"

"Not really, they make them with bourbon and call them Kentucky mules instead."

Current whistles long and slow. "How many is one too many?"

I laugh and follow him as he heads back out to his truck.

"One."

He reaches into the cab and then hands me a plastic box and a cup of coffee that doesn't feel very hot.

"The coffee's probably gone cold now," he apologizes, "but Millie will refill it for you as many times as you like if you're willing to hoof it over to the tavern."

The box appears to have pastries in it.

"Turn-overs aren't my forte," he mentions with a nod toward the box as he grabs some extra painting supplies from the bed of the truck, "but I'm working on it."

"You made these?"

When I get inside and get the lid off the box, I find an assortment of triangular pastries. I can plainly see the deep purple filling leaking from a couple and the apple ones have cute little heart cut-outs in the folded-over pie crust.

The purple ones are blackberry. I may be a mess

with powdered sugar all over my boobs and blackberry pie filling dribbling down my chin but I'm a happy mess. I don't even care that the coffee is cold.

"I'm still working on getting them folded so they don't fall apart so easy."

When I open my eyes, I see Current staring at me with heat in his eyes and I realize I was moaning.

It feels like a full minute that we stand there looking at each other and I'm pretty sure I'm not the only one thinking the painting can wait.

Current takes a step closer and swipes his finger along my jawline.

My nipples harden. My pulse quickens. I can't remember how to breathe.

"Sorry," he says, his voice low and husky, "they're kinda messy."

Then he licks the spilled filling off his fingers and steps out of my space. I'm breathing again but disappointment has left an ache between my legs.

"I was looking up small brewery operations online last night. What's your floor plan going to be like? We'll need to install floor drains...probably here, and here, at least..."

Current is walking the perimeter of the room, pointing out where the electrical already exists and talking about voltage and circuit breakers, plumbing and drainage, and asking me what kind of flooring I'm planning on going with.

"I figure leave the concrete bare back here, of course," he says, "but how much space are you dedicating to seating? Do you want to stain the concrete for that area or put down laminate of some sort?"

So much for fantasy time. I need to snap out of my daze and start putting some serious thought into how I'm going to make things work.

"I don't know," I tell him. "I have to have a kitchen now."

"Have to?"

"Yeah, I was on the phone all day yesterday getting all my applications settled and I woke up to an email this morning from the alcohol beverage board saying that I have to serve food if I'm going to sell alcohol."

"And I was thinking you were getting kicked by those mules in celebration," he jokes.

"I've been to Slow River," Current is saying as he holds one end of a tape measure while I try to re-imagine my entire plan. "Tapped Out doesn't have a kitchen."

"No, they have a fenced outdoor area where they can host catering trucks. I don't have any place I can do that here-- not to mention the fact that Moonshine Ridge doesn't exactly have a happening food truck scene."

"It has to be a full kitchen? You can't just like, get a couple of microwaves and serve Hot Pockets and frozen burritos?"

I drop the tape measure; I'm laughing so hard.

"You know? I'm not sure," I admit.

Current

Somehow, we manage to get some actual work done and by four o'clock, the walls are painted, and even though we still don't know how we're going to fit a commercial kitchen in the space, Ginger's mapped out where her brewing equipment has to go and I've marked the floor with masking tape to indicate where drains and outlets need to be put.

"Come up and I'll make you dinner."

We're putting supplies away after cleaning out brushes and tossing the rollers we won't need again. Spending the day with Ginger has been fun, we work well together. Thinking alike and able to play off one another whether we're joking around or solving puzzles to get her business up and running.

All the more proof that she's meant for me.

"Up?" She asks, confused.

"To my place," I explain, "on the river."

Ginger hesitates. It's after four in the afternoon on a weekday in October. The sun is already below the mountain range flanking the ridge on the west. It gets dark early this time of year up here, and I know she's got a two-hour drive back to the valley-- closer to three from Riverbend-- but if I have it my way, she won't be going home tonight.

"So you're saying that turnovers aren't the only thing you can make?"

The look on her face; she knows I'm hoping to make her more than dinner. I want to make her scream my name.

"I can make a lot more than dinner," I assure her. "Come on, follow me up the mountain and I promise you won't regret it."

"Said every ax-murderer ever," she teases.

I give her a shrug while I twirl my keys around my finger. "I'm really more of a chainsaw guy."

"You comin' or not?" I ask while she gathers her things and locks the door.

"Well, with both dinner and dismemberment on the table, how could I refuse?"

She makes me laugh. She also makes me feel a thousand things that are both scary as fuck and exciting as hell. Like running the class fours for the first time every spring when the river is new and even though I've done it a thousand times, it's different every year.

"I never dismember my victims on the same table I serve dinner on, it's not clean."

Now it's Ginger that's laughing.

We're standing face to face just outside the closed and locked door of Suite number eight.

Across the street Alice McAllister is glaring at us through the front window of her general store, Ash and Hyacinth's sporting goods place is already closed for the day, the tavern parking lot is filling up with pick-up trucks and SUVs for after work drinks and meals for anyone on the ridge that doesn't want to cook tonight.

The few businesses that share the building with Ginger are all locked up and dark, with the hanging lantern porch lights already glowing their warm yellow light along the boardwalk even though there's still plenty of light left from the fading day.

She's cute as hell, looking perfect with her hair twisted up in a messy bun that lost the fight against gravity about three hours ago. Now it's hanging loosely to one side of her head. There's a trace of mascara on those sandy blonde lashes today and, although she's still wearing clothes to paint in, I noticed a long time ago that there's a lacy, push-up bra under the simple gray t-shirt.

I want to tell her all the things I've been thinking since I met her a couple of days ago; how beautiful she is, how much I want to explore every sexy curve of her body, how she's going to be mine-- how I know that's true as sure as I know the way back to my own home.

Those gray eyes look up at me. There's still a smile on her face when she sees me looking down at her, but neither of us is laughing anymore.

Chapter Six

Ginger

Hell yeah, I'm going home with this man.

All day he's been making me laugh, keeping me from getting too deep in the stress. In between the suggestions of frozen pizza rolls and dinosaur chicken nuggets, he's had some good ideas as well, helping me brainstorm solutions every time I found another glitch in the floor plan.

He brought me breakfast, he's offering to make dinner for me, and... *that kiss!*

Off to my left, the sky over the mountains is putting on a show of pinks and oranges as the sun hits the horizon somewhere far beyond what's visible from the two-lane highway that's leading me to Current's place.

The tail lights of his truck lead the way, as he's careful not to get too far ahead of me.

I've been waiting for Current to kiss me all damn day. If he wasn't going to get around to doing it soon, I was going to have take matters into my own hands-- but it turns out, it's not that easy to get into a lip lock with a guy who's thirteen inches taller than you. Not in a room that doesn't have furniture, at least.

My lips are still tingling when we turn off the main road at the sign that says "Riverbend" hanging from a couple of wooden posts over the road. There's a canoe carved into the sign on one side and a kayak on the other.

Current told me his family runs a rafting company through the summer months, and almost the entire family has built houses on the property.

I love hearing him talk about his family. They sound a lot like my own; loud and messy and full of fun. I can't wait to meet them.

Because I don't think I'm imagining what's going on between us.

Something tells me that suite number eight isn't the only part of Moonshine Ridge that's going to be a big part of my future.

"Don't mind him," Current tells me when the soaking wet dog appears from nowhere. "That's Gopher, he won't bite but he will shake."

On cue, Gopher shakes and water goes flying in all directions. Including mine.

Before I have a chance to get properly introduced to Gopher, however, he's decided that his work here is done and heads off at a full run into the dim twilight.

"Sorry," Current says, but he doesn't look it at all. He's eyeing all places Gopher soaked my clothes through when I was trying to hug on him before took off, most of which are my boobs. "He's still just a pup, showed up a couple years ago or so and adopted us.

"Come on in, I'll find you something to change into. You can shower if you want."

Current's house is a basic rectangle built on a high deck. After following him up the steps from the gravel driveway, I get a quick tour: the deck wraps all the way around the house with the back built up on pilings sunk well into the riverbank below us. The house itself sports weathered wood siding and several large windows overlooking the river.

From the big set of sliding doors, Current hands me a t-shirt and a pair of sweatpants. The sliders open into a large living room with an open kitchen opposite and next to the front door.

Down the hall in one direction, is the master bedroom with the en suite.

Current doesn't follow me through the bedroom door.

"I'm going to get the oven going," he tells me, hovering in the hall just outside the doorway, "I'll have a cold beer for you when you're out-- if my brewbabe isn't too proud to drink mass produced swill, that is."

"Brewbabe?"

He shrugs, "seems fitting."

"None too proud," I assure him, "I'm a beer lover not a beer snob."

Current gives me a wink and a nod of his head but he doesn't head back to the kitchen right away and I wait for him to join me.

"OK then, see ya in a few."

"Yeah, sure, I'll be out quick."

I finally duck into the bathroom for a quick shower and that seems to break the spell that had Current rooted to the spot by the door.

His bathroom is nice, the shower is huge with tile all the way up the ceiling and a shower head placed high enough I can't reach it. He's six foot, four though. I'm guessing he had this custom built.

There's plenty of room in here for two and I stay under the hot water longer than just the few minutes it takes to rinse off the paint and the dog, thinking about what I might be doing right now if he'd joined me.

Current

The fire is going in the oven out on the back deck and I've got dough already rolled out and a variety of toppings at the ready when Ginger reappears.

Seeing her coming into the kitchen wearing one my *Jonesing for the River* t-shirts tied in a knot at her waist that pulls the worn, blue fabric tight across those magnificent tits of hers is enough to make me forget the words to the song I was just singing.

She obviously didn't see any point in putting her bra back on and I send a silent prayer to the heavens for the clear view of harden nipples straining against the material.

My old sweatpants are likewise transformed into something much sexier than I ever thought they could be. She's got the waist band rolled down so the pants sit low on those wide hips, putting a wide band of naked curves on display, revealing a pierced belly button and part of a tattoo peeking out from above the fuzzy gray lining of the sweats.

"Why'd you stop?" She asks.

"Huh?" My mind has gone blank. All I can do it stare at the swirls of blues and green and wonder what it leads to and where, exactly.

"That song," she tells me. "It's one of my faves."

"You know Cat Stevens?"

"Not personally," she scoffs. "I believe I was promised a beer."

Picking up Moonshadow back at the beginning, I grab a cold brew from the fridge for her and she sings along with me for a few lines before interrupting to ask me about dinner.

"What's going on here?" She motions the hand wrapped around a long neck bottle over my work station.

"Told you I'd make pizza." I grin as I step aside so she can get a better look at the two circles of dough I have rolled out and the choice of toppings.

"You just happen to have everything you could possibly need to make pizza at the ready?"

"Oven's up to temp too." I say proudly.

Her eyes dart to the obviously off and cold oven in the kitchen near the fridge.

I point out to the back deck.

"Come on, this one's yours," I slide one of the crusts toward her on the baking parchment, "this one's mine. Choose your weapons."

I motion at the toppings; a standard selection of red or white sauce, plus a jar of pesto; grated cheeses, meats, vegetables, sliced tomatoes. I even set out some pineapple chunks, just to see if she'd take the bait.

"What is this? Like a pizza death match?" She

sets her beer on the butcher-block top of my kitchen island and studies the options.

"You catch on quick."

She elbows me lightly, stepping into my space as she reaches for the pesto. Taking full advantage of my hesitation while I pause to breathe her in.

Her hair is damp and hanging loose down her back and she smells like my soap, my shampoo, and nothing at all like me. My dick is a steel rod under the sweats I threw on while she was in the shower.

With superhuman effort, I pull the end of my own t-shirt down and do the best I can to cover the evidence of my true intentions toward this beauty.

Then I reach for the white sauce and the fresh basil.

We go back to singing side by side while we each build our creations. Ginger's got a great singing voice. She's doing most of the heavy lifting in our duet.

"So seriously though," she says, pausing to sprinkle a touch of Italian seasoning blend over her finished pie and stepping back as if time just got called on one of those cooking competition shows, "how do you just happen to have an entire pizzeria's worth of fresh toppings?"

"Pizza's kinda my thing, I guess," I tell her, carrying hers out on a wooden board, letting her open the door for me.

"Vera and my mom did most of the cooking for

the overnight trips when I was still too little to go on the rafts. So I learned how to do all the camp cooking. A few years ago, Vera and Don retired from the outfit and I stepped in for the cooking duties.

"I can make pretty much anything on an open fire in a Dutch oven." I slide her pizza into the wood-fired, brick oven I built on the deck two years ago in the off season, then slip back inside and grab the other pie off the counter and add it to the oven too.

"Somebody on one of our week-long excursions a few years back was asking if it was possible to do pizza and I kinda went on a mission to perfect it. Built the brick oven out here a couple years ago now. I don't know-- some guys have a fridge full of burger makings, I have pizza toppings, I guess."

It only takes a couple minutes for these to cook through on the hot stone by the fire and I pull each finished pie out with the wooden peel. Setting them down on the patio table.

"We can eat out here if you want," I say, "while the fire's still going. Keep's the deck pretty nice this time of year."

"Sounds good," Ginger agrees.

Chapter Seven

Ginger

After dinner, we continue to argue over who made the better pizza while we sit on the deck and watch the river running under the moonlight.

Current's brick pizza oven provides some warmth in the cool fall air until the fire dies down.

"So what's this?" He asks, sliding a finger lightly along the edge of ink where his sweats don't cover my tattoo.

"Mermaid," I tell him but I don't offer him a better view of the tattoo that covers my entire hip and thigh down to my knee. I want him to kiss me again.

His fingers trace the design lower, pulling the

rolled fleece of the borrowed sweats down enough to uncover the siren's pink hair.

My skin burns where his fingers brush.

"Current." I whisper his name on a moan as his finger glides over the edge of my hipbone.

"Yeah?"

His lips are impossibly close to mine and the memory of how his mouth claimed mine momentarily before we left town has me leaning in, desperate to feel that hot possession again.

"I need you."

"Fuck. Ginger," he whispers against my lips, "I've needed you since the day I met you."

He seals his mouth against mine, our tongues tangling instantly.

The fingers that were so light against my skin just seconds ago are gripping my hip with an urgent command that pulls me closer till I twist beside him to straddle his lap.

Now I can feel his thick erection digging into the cleft of my pussy through the obstacle of our clothing. It's delicious torture, the way his hands move up, pulling the knot in the borrowed t-shirt loose so he can reach under it and cup my breasts in both hands.

The feel of callused hands against my skin has me grinding against him harder. His thumbs brush over my sensitive nipples, making me gasp.

"Like that?" His voice is a hoarse whisper

between kisses. He moves his thumbs again, slower and harder on my pebbled tips till I think I might come for him right now from that alone.

"Yeah," I answer, "how bout you?"

I slide my hands under his shirt and drag my fingertips over his chest. Letting the feel of his defined pecs caress my palms before finding his nipples and tracing them with my fingers.

Current inhales sharply and I know I've found a sensitive spot.

"You too, then," I murmur.

Pulling his shirt off over his head I bend to touch my tongue to one of the tightly puckered points. We go tumbling sideways together on the long, sectional outdoor sofa positioned not nearly close enough to the dying fire now.

Before I can get my mouth on him, though, Current rolls off the edge of the sofa and grabs me up in his arms.

"It's getting cold out here," he tells me, positioning me so that my legs wrap around his waist and I can feel that hard ridge of his against my core. "I want to know you're shivering because of me, not the chill in the air."

I cling to him as he carries me. One of his hands grips my ass as he opens the door and closes it after us.

Then both his hands are on my ass, his mouth is on mine again. Intensity blooms in the time it takes us to move from the front room to his bedroom.

By the time Current lays us both in the center of his big bed, I'm so desperate to feel him filling me up that it physically hurts to wait any longer.

"Uh uh," he says, grinning down at me, "Not before I get a good look at this mermaid."

He pulls my shirt off over my head and groans at the sight of my bare breasts. "Baby, these are magnificent." He sounds like he's admiring a priceless work of art.

Lowering over me, his mouth seers down my throat and over each breast, taking time to pay careful attention to my nipples till I'm writhing and mewling under him, begging for relief.

His fingers hook into the waistband of the pants and he pulls them over my hips and down my thighs slowly. Making sure his mouth covers every inch of skin exposed as he uncovers it.

"Damn baby," he inhales deeply as he reaches the space between my legs, "you smell like fucking heaven."

Current

Apparently, I'm not the only one who's had enough of the slow stuff.

With one final, harsh yank, I get the pants off her and tossed somewhere in a corner. My face is between those thick thighs of hers faster than she can get her last *"please"* out of her mouth.

Ginger's pussy has my mouth watering for more than just this taste of her. My cock is harder than I think it's ever been, leaking pre-cum and bobbing between my legs in anticipation.

Right now, I could probably just sink into the sweet, juicy pussy in front of me and put us both out of our misery. Ginger's so fucking wet for me and she hasn't stopped begging for my cock since we were dry humping on the patio.

God knows I'm about to burst from wanting to feel her warmth as it squeezes around my shaft.

First, I'm going to get my mouth on her and drink up some of her sweet nectar. The way she was on the edge already just from having me suck on those perfect tits of hers has me eager to find out how easy it's going to be to make her come on my face.

"OHMYGODCURRENT!"

Ginger's back arches, her fingers finding my hair and twisting into it as she bucks her hips off the mattress and fucks my face like I want her to.

I'd say a thousand filthy things to her right now if I didn't have my tongue buried in her hole with one thumb massaging her engorged clit while I hang on to her thighs for dear life.

My girl is just as wild as I expected her to be when I got in the sack. Ginger can't stay still and the way she's screaming for me has me glad I built my place with plenty of privacy.

Two fingers slip inside her, she's tight but she's so fucking wet that I can easily slide up to my last knuckle while I suck her needy clit.

"Please fuck me, Current." She says she's ready to get my dick inside her but she's not coming on my tongue yet. I can tell she's close though.

"Give me that cream first, baby." I tell her, replacing my mouth with my thumb long enough to tell her what I want from her. I keep finger fucking her with my other hand. "When this sweet little cunt of yours is coating my tongue with your cum, I'll give you my cock."

Her head thrashes against the bed and the string of words that are probably all curses come out garbled and breathy.

I drag the point of my tongue through her slick folds and flick it across her clit lightly. Ginger's movements become more intentional, she rides my beard and when I suck her little bud again, she explodes in an orgasm that has me fighting to keep control myself.

Fuck, she's gorgeous. Wild and untamed as her voice rings out over the sound of the river outside.

Her hips bucking as she grinds. A rush of hot fluid adds to her wetness as she gives me what I asked for and I lap up every drop.

Ginger's thighs go limp, falling open wide, and giving me a view of that glistening pussy. It's already deep pink from need and her inner thighs are pink from my beard.

I strip down in an instant and get between those creamy thighs with my throbbing cock fisted hard in my hand.

"Now, Current," she demands, "don't make me torture you back."

Just the thought of Ginger's smart mouth working my cock in a revenge blow job is powerful enough to make me lunge into her. If I didn't, I'd have sprayed her down in a really embarrassing lack of self-control just now.

"Holy shit, you feel good, baby," I gasp as my cock slides all the way home.

Ginger's tight tunnel pulls me deep, suctioning around me as our bodies become one. Nothing's ever felt as good as my woman's body welcoming me home right now.

White noise fills my ears and the beat of my own pulse hammers in my veins. The feeling is so intense I have to stop when I'm seated all the way to the root of my dick inside her.

"You OK?" I ask. I can feel her body already convulsing around me and she's shivering slightly even though her skin is hot and sweaty against mine.

"You're big," she says on a gasp that's part laugh. "It feels so...*full*."

Our foreheads meet and I give touch my lips to hers.

"Please fuck me, Current, fuck me like you own me."

"Oh baby," I growl as I pull back, "You know I do."

I thrust forward forcefully and Ginger grunts but her body begs for more. Soon we're in a race to see how fast we can get over that next cliff. I'm determined to push her over before I jump but I swear she's trying to make me lose control-- possibly consciousness.

Her walls tighten around me and I feel the flutters right before her channel clenches down on me.

Ginger screams my name and it's a call I can't resist this time.

Ropes of cum explode from me, coating her womb with my seed. It feels like forever till my cock stops going off inside her and I finally collapse across Ginger's body without an ounce of strength left in me.

Chapter Eight

Ginger

At some point we managed to get cold enough to get under the covers and make love again. When the sun's light filled the room early this morning, I made good on my threat to torture Current with my mouth.

When we'd laid in bed tangled up in each other's bodies long enough that we agreed we needed sustenance, he took me from behind while I leaned against the tiled wall of the shower with the water raining down on us from above.

My body is feeling sore and sated as I stand at the kitchen island with a hot cup of tea, made from herbs his grandmother grows in her garden, cupped between my hands.

Current flips chocolate, chocolate chip pancakes

on a griddle on his stove. He swears the chocolate pancakes are a perfect pairing for the sage and mint flavors of the tea and he is not wrong.

"So I was thinking," I muse between sips of the tea while I wait for another pancake to get delivered to the plate in front of me-- maybe I'll actually even put syrup on this one, but they don't need it.

"Me too," Current says.

He's wearing a pair of pajamas pants and an apron that ties behind his neck. His hair is still damp from our shower and it's drying in an uncombed mess. He's been singing broken bits and pieces of songs about sunshine all morning in an incomprehensibly bad medley.

"I should have probably asked you about a thousand questions last night before we got carried away," he tells me. He slides another pancake off the spatula onto my plate and then pulls me into an embrace that has me convinced I'm definitely not too sore for another round of that magic cock of his.

"But dammit, woman, you had me so wound up all night, if the cabin was under siege by bigfoots, I'd have still had to fuck you first."

He kisses me and goes back to his pancake project.

"Bigfoots? Not Bigfeet?" I ask.

"I'm pretty sure the appropriate plural is foots in this case," he says, thoughtfully.

"Is, um, Bigfoot likely to attack the cabin?"

"Nah, they're super shy." He says it dead seriously. "They try to avoid human contact at all costs, coming up to the house is a definite no go for our friendly skunk-apes."

When I don't respond, he turns to look at me. "What?"

"You're talking about Bigfoot as casually as you would talk about deer," I point out, "like you see them all the time or something."

Current flashes that panty-melting grin and laughs easily.

"Not all the time," he says, sliding another pancake in front of me, "but you don't live your whole life on this river without coming to understand why we have so many cyptos coming up here."

" 'Cryptos?' " It sounds like a cross between psychos and cryptocurrency.

"Cryptozoologists," he clarifies. "We get a lot of amateur Bigfoot hunters but we also get our fair share of legit scientists looking for proof of the species."

"You were talking about actually seeing Bigfoot?"

Current shakes his head and laughs. "No, I was talking about getting a ring on your finger and filling you up with babies."

"I'm pretty sure you were talking about Bigfoot."

I can feel myself blushing. Rings? Babies? Me? Callie might say his Bigfoot story is more believable.

But Callie doesn't know everything about me.

Something about the way Current is looking at me right now has my heart rate picking up, and not just because I can't help but get turned on every time he gives me that smile.

"Current, I'm opening a business. I'm not exactly at a place in my life to start popping out kids."

"Kinda one of the things we should have talked about before I dumped six gallons of cum in you, right?"

"Romantic," I scoff. "But I'm on birth control right now."

A darkness clouds his usually sunny features.

"Is there a reason you need to be on it?"

The possessive tone sends a shiver down my spine in a way I wouldn't expect. I like the way it makes me feel like I'm his.

"Not like you're thinking," I assure him. "But I am a twenty-five-year-old woman, Current."

"Ginger, I'm serious about what I said. I want to marry you. I want to have a family with you. If there's anyone else in the picture--"

"Oh wow." I practically purr the words even though I'm really surprised at myself as my body goes all liquid and buzzy again.

"What?" Current glowers.

"I just suddenly get why some girls go all stupid for that bossy caveman routine." I laugh feebly, I'm mostly just kinda turned on.

"There's no one else, Current. There hasn't been anyone else in my life in years, and there's never been anyone that made me feel the way I feel about you."

"Caveman, huh?"

Current

I never thought of myself as the jealous type, but the thought that Ginger might have something else going on had me ready to kill.

It helps that she assures me there's not. It helps more that she looks ready to jump me when she calls me "caveman."

"But what were you thinking about?" I bring the conversation back to where she started aways back now.

"Well, I was thinking that you should definitely dump more cum into me." It's fucking cute the way she makes air quotes when she says that. "And then, I was thinking that we could talk more about this ring and get on the same page with the baby timeline and then, I think I have a plan for the brewery that would give us enough space to put in a wood-fired pizza oven...if you'd be willing to train a cook for me."

"Hell no!" I say it forcefully enough to make

Ginger flinch, and the look of disappointment on her pretty face has me quick to gather her up in my arms.

"I'm not training anyone. I'll be the god ruling your pizza oven by day and the god ruling your body at night."

"That's pretty cheesy," she tells me, wrapping her arms around my waist.

"You liked the caveman thing better?" I quirk an eyebrow.

"It might have been hotter than it should be," she admits.

"Ugh!" I grunt in mock-caveman speak, "Wohman. Mine. Fuck now."

Ginger laughs her head off as I bend down and toss her over my shoulder. Making sure the stove's turned off before hauling her playful ass back to bed while she pretends to fight back. I'm sure she's pretending because her hands are all over my ass.

"Marry me." I try saying it with this newfound caveman tone but I'm still trying to catch my breath.

"Of course, I'm going to marry you," Ginger's breathing just as hard as I am.

We're both flat on our backs on the rumpled bed

sheets that we hadn't put back in order from this morning, sticky from sweat and orgasms.

"Current Jones, I knew you were the man I was going to spend my life with the day you walked in while I was painting the ceiling." Ginger rolls over on her side to face me, her fingers skip lightly over my chest and draw little spirals over my skin.

"When do we start making babies?" I would breed her tomorrow if she was ready, but I'm willing to do a few practice runs first if that's what my woman wants.

"How about, we get the brewery open first?"

"I can work with that timeline. When do you want to get married?"

Ginger laughs. "I'm not going anywhere, Current. I'm yours."

"And I'm yours." I roll us over and kiss her deeply. "I'm not trying to keep you from getting away, I just love you and I want us to start our life together."

"I love you too," Ginger says, her fingers reaching up to touch my face. "Our life together started the minute I saw you."

Epilogue 1
One Week Later

Ginger

"**G**inger!"

Anise Jones practically accosts me, wrapping me in a tight hug while Current takes a step back and lets his mom squeeze the breath out of me.

Bank, Current's dad steps in next with a quicker, less suffocating embrace. "Beer?" he asks, when he releases me.

"Got it, Dad," Current hands me bottle from an ice chest sitting by the back door of his parents' house.

Apparently Bank and Anise are the usual hosts of family gatherings, even though two out of three of Current's brothers also live on the property, as well as Vera and Don.

Speaking of whom: Grandma V, as Current tends to call her-- everyone else just calls her by her first name-- sweeps out of the back door from the kitchen in a flurry of long skirts and a thick, multi-colored sweater suitable for the chilly October night.

"Sweetheart," she pulls me into a one-armed embrace. "Oh good, they gave you one of the good beers. How have you been?"

I got to meet Vera a few days ago when I stayed over with Current after a long night working on the brewery. She's exactly the way Current described her-- an eighty-year-old hippy, complete with feathers in her hair. Today it looks like it might be a wild turkey feather, but I haven't learned my local birds yet.

"I'm good," I promise her, "I like your sweater."

"Mable made it," she tells me with pride, "she's going to stop by later. Be warned, she'll probably bring Jell-O."

"Don't eat Mable's Jell-O," Current swoops by to kiss me and whisper words of caution in my ear before heading into the kitchen to graze on the tray of fresh veggies that his mom set out for everyone.

Curiosity about Mable's gelatin of doom aside, the Jones family is easy as easy to fall in love with as Current.

Since I'm the oldest of five myself, this feels a lot like home and I can't wait till I get to introduce

Current to my own family of crazy characters back in Slow River.

That's going to be a couple of weeks from now though. We're working hard to get me moved up to Moonshine Ridge while we also get started on the final plans for the Brick and Porter, the name Current and I picked out for my-- *our*-- new taphouse and pizza parlor, now that we know exactly what we need to make it work.

After a week of planning and talking, we've decided to get married up here at Riverbend early next summer. Late May, before the family's river season kicks off in full swing and-- crossing my fingers-- after Brick and Porter has its official opening.

"Give me back my girl, Grandma," Current drops a kiss on his grandmother's cheek as he pulls me out from under her arm. "It's time for the ceremonial lighting of the Q," he explains, dropping his arm over my shoulders as everyone who was inside makes their way out to the back patio where Bank stands beside the humongous gas grill, his finger poised on the ignition switch.

Apparently, lighting the grill is a whole thing to these people.

The gas burners ignite with a slight whoosh and the crowd goes wild.

"I don't get it," says the young boy standing with Rapid. "What's the big deal?"

Rapid is the oldest of the Jones brothers; not as tall as my six-foot, four fiancé, but wider at the shoulders, longer in the beard, and seems to wear a perpetual scowl. He doesn't seem to talk much, and I only just met him for the first time earlier this afternoon when he was giving lessons on how to use a kayak paddle to Jackson.

About everyone around us laughs and I notice even Rapid cracks a smile as he explains that his dad couldn't get his first gas grill lit for well over an hour and so it just became a thing for everyone to gather around to watch Bank light the grill now.

Eight-year-old Jax still doesn't get the big deal and heads for the kitchen where the snacks are.

"What's going on there?" River, Current's youngest brother asks Rapid as Jax disappears inside. "This is like the third time you've brought the kid up here."

"Just teachin' him how to paddle while the river's calm," Rapid gruffs at the younger man. "Don't start making up stories about it."

"Hey!" Current shouts, gathering everyone around us before the crowd has a chance to disperse. "Don't go anywhere just yet, we have an announcement."

A couple of brothers groan.

"You guys remember what I said last time we got together?" Current asks, rhetorically, "This is Ginger-- my *fiancée*."

"Fiancée? You just met her a week ago, man!" Rapid says.

"It took you a whole week?" Eddy jokes, pulling his very pregnant wife into a tight hold beside him. "I got my ring on Pepper in four days!"

Pepper holds up her hand with all five digits on display and mouths "five" at me.

Bank stands by his grill and pulls Anise closer to him. "You boys are taking things slow," he says proudly, "I had your mother at the alter--"

"In less than twenty-four hours," the entire family choruses.

The rest of the night is all laughter, good food, and stories of Current growing up as his family members take turns trying to embarrass him.

It's chaos, and I love it.

Epilogue 2
Six Months Later

Current

"Ready?"

Ginger takes a deep breath and nods.

"This sucks," she says, placing a hand over her growing bump and rubbing, "Award-winning brew-mistress that can't drink at my own grand opening."

My wife likes to give me shit for knocking her up but she's not fooling me or anyone else. She was so excited about that plus sign on the home pregnancy test that she knocked me down when she jumped on me with the news as soon I walked through the door that day.

That was five months ago, just a week after we got her out of her place down in Slow River and officially moved in with me. Guess her birth control was no match for my super swimmers.

It is kinda ironic though; Ginger's porter just won a national competition and she can't even celebrate the realization of her dream with a proper pint.

"I promise to drink for both of you," I lay a kiss on those sweet lips of hers and try to behave myself.

We have most of Moonshine Ridge outside waiting for Sheriff Hawkins to cut the ribbon that's been tied across our door so we can start pouring flights and building pizzas.

It's small space for the crowd outside but the sheriff and Mable Hart agreed to let us expand onto the boardwalk porch under the awning for one night only.

The brick pizza oven is hot and ready and since the April afternoon is still crisp with a thin layer of snow lying on the ground around town, we have the fire in the fireplace stoked as well.

The final floor plan allowed for a long bar that separates the open kitchen from the dining area, a few tables against the wall in the back of the room, and instead of tables and chairs, we opted for cozy, open seating that can be moved as needed so people can gather around the fireplace at the front of the restaurant.

Cedar McAllister and his wife even closed up their tavern across the street this afternoon so they can support our opening.

That's the kind of community spirit you find in a

place like Moonshine Ridge and I'm proud as fuck of my hometown showing up to support my wife like they have.

"You guys ready?" Hawk pokes his head through the door, a pair of ceremonial, oversize scissors in his hand.

One more look at Ginger and I nod when she gives me the OK.

"Ladies, Gentlemen, kin-folk, and drunkards!" Hawk stands on the edge of the boardwalk and shouts above the crowd, "As deputy sheriff, and having been voted the closest thing Moonshine Ridge has to a mayor, I'd like to welcome you all and thank you for turning out to support our newest addition to the community-- our very own craft brewery and pizza joint. I hereby declare Brick and Porter Pizza and Brewing open for business!"

Hawk works the cardboard scissors and the ribbon breaks clean along the place it was conveniently perforated.

The ribbon cutting tools were provided courtesy of Mable and Grandma V who found them online. No one can remember the last time a business opened on the ridge-- aside from Howard's hookah shop, that is.

People flood through our doors, shaking hands with me and Ginger, congratulating us on the new business, the new baby, and our upcoming wedding next month where we're sure to see most of the same faces again.

Cami volunteered to help pour beer flights which we are doing at half-price so everyone gets a taste of what's on tap, and Mom and Dad are taking orders for pizza and helping with the assembly process.

"Looks like I'm on duty, baby," I give Ginger a kiss and head for the oven. I can see Mom's already got a line of pies ready to go in and I don't want to get backed up on opening day.

"You want ginger-ale or root-beer, bud?" Rapid asks, Jax as they push past me with barely a wave as Sage stops to hug Ginger on her way in.

By the time the crowd thins around ten at night, we've already changed out kegs a few times and run out of the pre-rolled crusts I'd prepared for our opening-- which means we're about twenty-five pizzas over our high estimate.

We've taken down a lot of suggestions-- mostly "bigger beer glasses," and "bigger pizzas," and two tip jars crammed full of loose change and bills.

Ginger sends one of the tip jars home with Cami for all her help, and tries to push one on Mom and Dad but they manage to sneak out without taking it with them.

Grandma V and Mable Hart are sitting in the far back table with an empty pitcher of Ginger's "Mad as Hell IPA" and a half-eaten pizza between them

Driven to the Mountain

and they are cackling in the way that only scheming old ladies can.

"Can we make sure Vera and Mable get home safe?" I elbow Hawk and nod toward my grandmother and her friend. "I'd like to get through our grand opening without having to bail Grandma V out of jail."

Hawk is the new sheriff deputy assigned to the ridge. He took over for Eric last month when Eric took a position as sub-sheriff down at the county offices and moved to Slow River.

The deputy stares at what I'm sure look like two, innocent, little old ladies to him. Poor guy's not from the ridge originally. He doesn't know he's looking at two of Moonshine Ridge's most notorious criminals.

"Yeah, sure," he says nonchalantly.

"Don't listen to either one of them if they say anything about visiting a friend on the way home."

"I got this handled," Hawk assures me. "You get your wife home and keep her off her feet for a while. I think I can handle of a couple of tipsy old ladies."

Hawk rounds up the old ladies in question and loads them into his SUV while Ginger and I lock up for the night.

"He knows not to let them talk him into any detours, right?" Ginger asks as she watches the sheriff's vehicle pull out of the parking space in front of our building.

"Nope. I tried to warn him, but I can already tell he's going to have to learn the hard way."

Ginger tucks herself under my arm as we walk to my truck, her hands are already making it clear exactly how she expects to celebrate our successful opening when we get home and my cock is in full agreement.

If they end up in jail this time, someone else is going to have to worry about it.

Called to the Mountain

About

Rapid Jones

Moonshine Ridge never had a doctor when I was growing up. Anything that Mom couldn't fix with a bandage and a kiss meant a drive down to the clinic in the valley.

Now one of the big medical groups has built a rural clinic with living quarters attached for the doctor they've stationed here.

Never paid much attention till the night I have to drag my buddy out of a bar fight with a busted nose.

When we hit the emergency call ringer on the clinic door, I'm not prepared for the woman that answers.

A single mom with a new medical license, determined to make a better life for herself and her son here in the mountains; Sage Everett is all business...but she's also all woman.

She needs a man who will prove to her that she deserves to be loved, and her son needs to know what a father is supposed to be.

I know I'm that man for both of them but Sage isn't quick to trust again and she's giving me an ache that no prescription can cure-- I won't be well until I can convince Doctor Everett to kiss it and make it better.

Welcome to Moonshine Ridge and the rugged wilderness surrounding the remote mountain community where the history is long, the local lore is deep, and the men are as wild as the mountains they come from.

Protective, possessive, totally obsessed; the men of Moonshine Ridge will do anything necessary to claim the women they love and give her the happily ever after she deserves.

The Moonshine Ridge books contain a lot of insta-love, some swearing, some steamy scenes, zero cheating, and a lot of swoon-worthy happy endings. They're interconnected with recurring characters but can be read as stand-alones in any order.

Copyright © 2023 Rocklyn Ryder

All rights reserved worldwide
No part of this book may be reproduced, uploaded to the Internet, or copied without permission from the author. The author respectfully asks that you please support artistic expression and help promote anti-piracy efforts by purchasing a copy of this book at the authorized online outlets.

This is a work of fiction intended for mature audiences only. Names, characters, places, and incidents either are the product of the author's imagination or are used fictitiously. Any resemblance to events, locales, business establishments, or actual persons, living or dead, events, or locales is purely coincidental.

Chapter One

Sage

"Do you have everything?"

Jackson lifts his arm with the small backpack that Rapid bought for him for their weekend camping trip. My son rolls his eyes at me and tips his head to one side in exasperation.

"You packed your river shoes?" I ask.

"Mom! I got everything, okay?"

"Sunscreen? Bug spray? Did you remember your toothbrush?"

My eight-year-old son huffs at me impatiently but he sets the pack down and opens it up so I can go through the check list myself.

"Rapid said if I forget something, he'll have spares," Jackson says, sounding for all the world like I'm being entirely unreasonable.

"He's not going to have spare underwear in your size." I think I'm making sense; my son begs to differ.

"Mom." Jackson pulls the backpack from me and refastens the zippers and straps. "It's a *guys'* weekend."

"So, you don't need underwear?"

He rolls his eyes at me again. Obviously, I just don't understand what it means to have a *"guys' "* weekend.

Rapid Jones has been such a great influence on Jackson; helping with school projects and spending the summer teaching him the basics of canoeing and kayaking, but this is the first time I've agreed to let Rapid take Jax for a whole weekend and it's true that I might be a tad extra with the mothering.

A knock on the door to the private entrance of our house that connects to the part of the building that serves as a small medical clinic here in Moonshine Ridge has Jackson grabbing the little pack and hoisting it onto his slim shoulders.

He's been practicing ever since Rapid brought it over a few weeks ago.

I didn't even know they made backpacks like that for kids. It's not a regular backpack with superheroes printed on it for hauling books and cold lunches to school, it's an honest-to-gosh backpacking pack. The kind designed for carrying life-sustaining gear on multi-day hikes into the wilderness.

Jax loves it.

Jax loves Rapid.

"Hey Rapid!" Jackson pulls the door open with more force than necessary then immediately calms to a guy-appropriate coolness. He exchanges an elaborate, multi-step handshake with the man standing on our front porch while I stand here just waiting till my ovaries stop exploding.

"Hey man, you got everything?"

The deep rumble of Rapid's voice sends a few more sparks through the ovaries and settles as a pool of warmth between my legs.

Jackson twists his body to show off the backpack. "Check!" he assures the older man.

"Why don't you go throw your pack in the truck while I talk to your mom?"

With a salute, my son pushes past Rapid's legs and darts out to the lifted four by four diesel sitting behind my little hatchback in the driveway.

"Did he really get it all?" Rapid's voice morphs from the child-appropriate bro tone he uses with Jax to that deep purr he uses with me. The one that has me pressing my thighs together to relieve the pressure that always builds when his attention is on me and me alone.

"I think so," I answer, willing my body to calm in his presence so I can adapt the *just Jackson's mom* demeanor that I've determined is the safest way to interact with this man. After all, Rapid has taken my son under his wing and given him the outlet for all that eight-year-old boy energy he needs as well as the male role model he's been lacking, but he's never indicated that he sees me as anything other than *just Jackson's mom* and the doctor in residence for the sleepy mountain community.

"He wouldn't let me go through everything," I say, "but I'm pretty sure he has the basics at least. If he forgot something I can always--"

Rapid flashes a rare grin. It's the kind that's genetically predisposed to dropping panties and the effect is only intensified considering how rarely he uses it.

His hand raises in the air and waves away my words.

"It's a short paddle up river and a day at camp before we paddle back. All he really needs is a sleeping bag and spare set of clothes if he ends up in the water. I got extra everything if he forgot something."

"I just want to make sure he's got everything he needs," I protest, "you already do so much for him. I don't want him to be burden."

"Sage--"

My thighs quiver every time this man calls me by my first name. It took months to get him to stop calling me "Doctor Everett." Sometimes I think I should have let him keep addressing me professionally, something about the way my name sounds coming from those full lips always makes me imagine what it would sound like if he said it when we were--

"-- I have three younger brothers and I've been leading youth outings since I was sixteen. This is not my first rodeo. I'm a certified lifeguard with swift water rescue training and I'm certified in CPR.

"We'll be fine. And I promised Jax I'd take him on an overnight if he aced that summer reading challenge. I owe the kid."

"I just appreciate all you've done for Jackson," I tell him, "He's really getting attached to you and your family and I don't want him wearing out his welcome is all."

Rapid gives me a look that I'm not sure I've ever seen on him before. For a second, he looks like a man on the verge of making a confession. Then the expression passes and his face is stretched in that wide grin that shines from under the beard that covers his face.

"Not a chance in hell of that happening," he assures me. "You get the weekend off, right?"

"As much as a small-town doctor with no relief ever gets a weekend off." I laugh.

"Well, the biggest trouble-makers on the ridge are going to be on a weekend canoe trip, so things should be quiet enough around here for the next few days. Oughta give you a chance to take a bubble bath. Have a glass of wine-- or three. Read one of those sappy romance books with all the filthy parts left in."

Is that fire I see in those blue eyes?

He's probably just getting a kick out of making me blush.

"How do you know what I have planned for my weekend?" I duck out from under his gaze, making busy work for myself by rearranging the stems of late season wild flowers in the bouquet on the table.

Rapid's smile become a light laugh as he shakes his head, "I know what Mom did whenever she got us boys out of the house."

"Rapid! Are we going?" Jackson's voice is all eagerness and impatience as he yells from the driveway.

"On it, bud!" Rapid yells back. "I'll have him back on Sunday afternoon," he says, turning back to me.

"You boys have fun." I follow him to the front door so I can wave goodbye. I've already extorted two hugs and a kiss from Jax and I know how far I'll get if I expect another one in front Rapid.

Rapid lingers on the porch for a moment and I think how I wouldn't mind a goodbye kiss from him too. With those deep blue eyes surrounded by sandy lashes and the crinkles at the corner of his eyes that tell the tale of his life outdoors; the cropped, blonde hair with the playful cowlick hanging over his eyes and that bushy mountain man beard that looks like it would be so soft against my face with his lips on mine.

"See ya later, Doc." My fantasy winks and bounces out to the driver's side of the truck at a jog.

"Bye Mom!" Jackson's tiny hand waves frantically through the open passenger side window as they pull out of the drive and disappear up the main road, into the mountains that surround the populated area of Moonshine Ridge.

Rapid Jones is quickly turning into more than just a passing fantasy for me. I've officially developed a crush.

Rapid

As expected, Jax didn't even make it to s'mores our first night. Paddling up-river is hard work, even after thirty years since my own first up-river trip with Grandpa Don when I was six.

After a few hours of doing my best to let Jax hold his own against the current, I dug in and got us to camp when I saw the kid was losing steam. He caught his second wind when we pulled the boat on shore and set up the tent but by the time I had supper cooked on the camp stove, I had to wake him up to eat, then he promptly crawled into the tent and crashed hard.

That leaves me alone in front of the fire, toasting marshmallows for one and leaving my mind free to wander.

It's easy to love Jackson. The kid is all the best things I remember about being that age myself, curious, strong-willed, and determined to establish his own identity.

But what I really want is his mom.

Letting the marshmallow on the end of my whittled stick catch on fire, I feel my features set in a thoughtful scowl as I watch the sugary torch flare for a few seconds.

My brothers tell me I do it wrong-- River will spend hours carefully turning a marshmallow above the flames until it's evenly toasted on all sides to a golden brown.

I never had that kind of patience. Stick the thing in the fire and light it up. Who cares about a little char on the outside when you get the perfect, molten middle in mere seconds? Of course, I've lost more than one marshmallow in the fire over the years as they ooze off of sticks and skewers before I can pull them from the flames.

This one makes it out of the fire and onto the Graham cracker.

I wonder if Sage has ever made s'mores.

The doc is a city girl, born and bred. She only

moved up to the ridge a little over a year ago when some big medical group funded a long over-due rural clinic for our remote mountain town, complete with the on-site, live-in, sexy-as-fuck Doctor Everett and her son.

I've been obsessed since I got my first good look at her: It was the end of the season last year. My family's river touring business had hung up the annual "closed for season" signs and all the boats and gear was in storage. I finally had some free time to get into town, have a few drinks with the guys and let loose.

Till dumbfuck Hayle put his hands on the new waitress down at the tavern and got his nose busted for it.

Fucker deserved it too.

Over the years that we've been buddies, I've watched Hayle get better and then get worse again. He's my friend and I'll always have his back, but when he pulled that stunt down at the tav, I knew it was time to let him suffer his own consequences.

That, and there was no way I was stepping between Cedar McAllister's fist and Hayle's face that night, man. You don't fuck with a woman that's been claimed by a mountain man. Hayle had that hit coming.

I think about Sage. How I'd react if anyone messed with her. I'd kill the fucker. Drop his body off a cliff up here in the mountains so high the animals would have his bones picked cleaned before anyone found them.

Not that she knows how I feel about her. I've been real careful to keep my feelings hidden from her and everyone else, but I've been obsessed with Doc Everett ever since she answered that after-hours emergency call button I pushed at damn near midnight while Hayle's nose was gushing so much blood I couldn't tell if it was that or the alcohol that had him near passed out.

She came to the clinic door with the kind of awareness that comes from a shot of pure adrenaline getting pumped into your bloodstream when your body is still dead asleep. Her hair was a mess of sleep-matted, dark waves falling down all the way to middle of her back.

Her face was scrubbed free of makeup and bore the tell-tale lines of having been pressed to a pillow very recently, and the lab coat hastily thrown on over the simple pink pajamas hadn't hidden the curves that were displayed in a way that her usual uniform of scrubs never showed.

I could have taken her right there that night. She was the most beautiful woman I'd ever seen and all I wanted to do was leave Hayle bleeding on the clinic's doorstep while I pushed her inside and fucked her on the exam table.

Of course, I put my reaction down to the booze we'd been slinging all night and the fact that it's been a long ass time since I've taken a woman to bed; the adrenaline of the fight and trying to get Hayle's bleeding to stop.

Watching her handle the emergency situation with Hayle, getting the bleeding stopped and finding a local ride to get him to the emergency room in Slow River quicker than an ambulance could have, only managed to get me more interested.

Interested enough to find half a dozen excuses to stop by the clinic over the next few months after that night.

Allergy meds, a tetanus shot for a scratch I'd gotten repairing a fence on the property, butterfly bandages on a cut that I'd normally have washed with soap and water and thrown a piece of tape over.

Every time I saw her, she was more beautiful than the time before. Always remembering to ask about Hayle-- even though no one's heard from that asshole since he left the ER in Slow River-- always remembering anything I'd told her on a previous visit, asking about my family, our river guide business, my dumb ass brothers falling head over heels and getting married without taking a breath between "will you" and "I do."

That thought has me deepening my frown and shaking my head. The movement is enough to send my current marshmallow dripping off the end of the stick and flaring up as it hits the burning log that's fueling the fire.

I'd finally screwed up the nerve to ask her out on a proper date. I couldn't take any more of the burning need for the woman that had been building up inside of me for months and I was determined to find out if it was just lust that I needed to get out of my system or if maybe there might be more to this one.

That was the day I met Jax.

Sage and I were standing at the reception counter in the tiny lobby of the clinic, bullshitting about God knows what while I tried to screw up my courage to ask her out when the kid came barreling through the door from their private residence, fit to be tied over some science fair project he couldn't get to work.

Till then, I didn't have a clue that Doc was a single mom.

Everything changed for me in that instant. She doesn't need some bearded yokel sniffing her panties, she needs a man. For her boy and for herself. Someone who's going to show up for them. Every time.

Well, it was easy enough to come back by with the stuff needed to help Jackson out with his project and after spending a few hours with him, I was smitten.

The kid needs a man in his life. Especially if he's

going to grow up here on the mountain. He'll need someone to teach him how life up here is different than in the city, and I'm more than up to that challenge.

But it sure as fuck complicates my feelings for Sage.

Dropping the stick I whittled to a point into the fire, I watch as it burns down before I douse the fire and crawl into the tent myself.

No doubt Jax will be as bright-eyed and bushy-tailed as ever at the first hint of dawn, and I promised pancakes and bacon for breakfast.

From what I've learned, Jackson's dad isn't in the picture much and Sage isn't ready to put her heart on the line again just yet.

So even though it gets harder to resist claiming her every passing day, I'm fighting the temptation to loosen that long, dark hair and see it fall over those curves while I make her mine; because when I finally do, it's going to be for keeps.

Chapter Two

Sage

"...And then Rapid had to jump in the river to get us unstuck and..."

Jackson hasn't stopped talking since he got out of the truck before Rapid even had the engine turned off.

"Rapid jumped in the river?" My eyes fly to Rapid, filled with questions.

He shakes his head slowly and rolls his eyes, letting me know that the daring tale of white-water rescue that my son is telling is laced with more than a little hyperbole.

"It's late in the season, the river is low. We got beached on a sandbar," Rapid clarifies.

"The water was moving so fast, Mom!" Jackson's hands wave frantically, emulating his version of the river's current. "There were rapids everywhere and we had to go right over them!"

Rapid holds up a single finger above Jackson's head and mouths, "Class one," silently.

I don't really know what class one rapids are, but if Rapid thinks it's safe for Jackson, then I trust him. Rapid would never put Jackson in danger, I know that.

"Hey bud," Rapid puts his hand on Jackson's head and tousles his hair, "why don't you bring in your pack so we can get your clothes in the wash while you shower up?"

Jackson runs back out to the truck and Rapid moves closer to the kitchen where I'm pulling the makings for hamburgers from the fridge.

"You're staying for dinner, right?" I ask, trying not to sound too hopeful.

"Um, sure, I guess I can do that." Rapid reaches into a cabinet for a glass and fills it with water from the tap.

"I'm sure you two subsisted off of cold toaster pastries and marshmallows all weekend," I tease, "you're probably starved for real meat."

Rapid leans back against the kitchen counter and sips from the glass. I love that he's become such a fixture around the house and that he's comfortable enough to make himself at home here, but the kitchen is barely big enough for one person as it is, adding Rapid's six foot, one inches of wide-shouldered, muscular frame doesn't just cramp the small space, it makes it damn near impossible for me to concentrate on anything other than his presence.

The space between his eye brows deepens into a crease that's been worn in permanently from the scowl he seems to wear most of the time. At first, I thought he was just mad all the time, but I've come to understand that his harsh expression is born of deep thought and careful observation.

He takes another sip of water and watches me arrange fresh fixings for burgers on the counter. After an intense moment of silence that has me feeling hot and bothered and hoping my bra covers the hardening of my nipples, Rapid sets the glass down, rolls up his sleeves, and washes his hands thoroughly.

"We heated beans on the fire and ate them from the can like men," he tells me. "In the morning, we foraged for wild berries and drank coffee we'd brewed overnight in our boots."

"Remind me never to go camping with you."

We laugh easily. Rapid finds a bowl and mixes the ground beef with seasonings and forms patties for burgers while I wash lettuce and slice tomatoes.

By the time we have everything ready to assemble, Jackson has joined us after a shower and a phone call to one of his school friends to report on his weekend.

"And Rapid made pancakes and bacon *on the*

fire, Mom." Jax says around a mouthful of burger. "And he brought these packs for dinner that had everything already in them-- even vegetables-- and we just put them in the fire to cook and ate out of the foil packets like real mountain men."

He slurps down some milk between bites of food and more enthusiastic accounts of the weekend. Going on to talk about Rapid's incredibly barbaric method of roasting marshmallows and finishing with a Bigfoot sighting.

Rapid smiles as he chews and shakes his head again.

"It was a deer," he says after swallowing.

"It could have been a Bigfoot though," Jackson turns to Rapid and tells him insistently. "You said you've seen him there before."

"But not this time of year," Rapid says matter-of-factly. "We wouldn't have camped in his turf when he needs it."

"No worries," Rapid turns to tell me, "the 'Squatches live on a migratory path, it's not the season for them up here right now."

"I'm just going to leave it alone that you're talking about Sasquatch as casually as you would deer or raccoons." I've heard more than one resident of Moonshine Ridge talk about the local "skunk ape" population like they're real. I'm not one to dismiss the possibility, but I have a feeling that Moonshine Ridge enjoys its reputation for being home to one of the most active populations of the elusive-- and probably mythical-- beasts.

"Crashed," I tell Rapid with a smile as I return from Jackson's suddenly all-too-quiet bedroom where he disappeared shortly after dinner.

"A couple days on the river will do that to you." He grins and helps me clean up from dinner.

"You don't seem any worse for wear," I point out, stacking dishes in the sink and running the hot water.

"I've been paddling since I was big enough to sit in grandpa Don's lap in the canoe."

"Oh no," I say, quickly stopping him from filling the dishwasher, "it's not working."

The zing of electricity that shoots through me when my hand lands on his bulging bicep makes me stumble slightly. How can those muscles be so huge when he's not even flexing?

That crease between Rapid's eyebrows deepens, the corners of his lips down-turned as he looks at me.

"Isn't that the clinic's responsibility? They're the ones who provide your housing, right?"

I shrug as I wash the dishes by hand, Rapid easily falling into the routine beside me to rinse and dry them.

"I put in a call for maintenance, but it's not considered a priority. You know how hard it is to get people up to the ridge," I explain as we work side by side.

Rapid has the sleeves of his flannel shirt rolled up to his elbows, putting muscled forearms on display while he helps with the dishes. The sight has me giddy, my mind racing with filthy thoughts of what those strong hands could do to me. I'm way too old to be swooning like a love-struck teenager over the sight of a man's forearms, for fuck's sake!

Still, this man makes me feel things I've never felt before. I thought chemistry like this only existed in movies and books. I just wish he felt it too.

"I have some wine left over from the weekend," I tell him, feeling shy about the memories of how I spent my weekend thinking about him. "Care to help me finish it off?

Rapid

The chains on the porch swing creak softly as I rock us gently. It's been hung high and Sage's feet don't even touch the ground, but my boots rest flat on the paving stones beneath the swing.

"So, whatever happened to your friend?" Sage

asks, settling onto the bench beside me close enough I can feel her beside me. "The guy with the broken nose-- Hayle?"

"No clue." I shrug and sip at the red wine she poured for us. "He disappeared right after that. His folks say he put most of his stuff in storage in their garage and even they haven't heard much from him."

"You've mentioned he was trouble," she says, her arm brushing mine when she lifts her glass to her lips. The gentle contact sends sparks flying through me and I'm glad for the low light from the solar lanterns out here and the untucked shirt-tails of my flannel that help hide her effect on me.

"You don't seem like the kind of man who would put up with a guy like that," she says after another sip of wine, "how'd you end up friends with him?"

"The ridge is small," I tell her. "Our grandparents were close so our parents are kinda close. I grew up with the Hart kids; but Hayle and I didn't get to be close till after his dad died. I guess, we're both the oldest in our family's and I could see how the pressure to grow up before he was ready was affecting him. He needed a friend."

Sage nods beside me and I fight the urge to turn toward her. I want to see her face, watch her thoughts show in her expression, but I know if I face her while we're sitting so close like this, it'll be too easy to press my lips to hers.

"So--" I clear my throat and shift slightly, trying to adjust my hard-as-a-rock dick behind my zipper without being obvious. "Jax says his dad's going to come pick him up and take him to the coast next week."

Sage makes a noise that sounds like my grandmother when she digs up a carrot that the rabbits have gotten to from underground.

"Yeah, Jackson's never been to the ocean so Arnold promised he'd take him."

"That's nice," I say, impressed. From what I gathered; Sage's ex hasn't been much for keeping up with his visitation plans.

Sage harrumphs in the dark at my side and I wonder if there's more to the story than she's telling me.

"We'll see," she says quietly into her wine glass.

"So, what happened with Jackson's dad and you?" I'm not sure I want to hear this, but I need to know she's not still in love with the guy. "You've never really told me how you two ended up here on the ridge. Alone."

"I went back to get my license," she says simply. "Turns out, he didn't think *doctor* was an appropriate profession for a woman."

"Girls are nurses, boys are doctors?" I know that type. Fucking idiots.

"I was already in medical school when we met," she continues with a nod, "he knew what my plans were. Turns out, he thought medical school was just a way to get--"

"Your MRS degree?" Now I do turn toward her, desperate to see her face and I'm not surprised to see the look of disgust twisting her pretty lips.

"Pretty much. He love-bombed me from the beginning-- my apartment was wall to wall flowers for months. Fancy dinners, jewelry...but the thing that fooled me was that he acted like he actually supported my career goals. Till we got married."

"What changed?" If she tells me hit her, I'll kill him.

Sage must hear it in my tone because she quickly assures me that wasn't the case.

"No, nothing so overt. That would be have been easy to catch. I was so close to finishing everything and getting my medical license. He talked me into postponing it for the wedding, insisting on a big, fancy event that took over a year of planning.

"My plan was to go back and take my exams when we got back from the honeymoon but then he started talking about starting a family."

Sage sighs deeply and it's plain as day that that was something she wanted badly.

"I wanted to wait a year, but Arnold knew I wanted a big family. He kept pointing out that I was already in my late twenties and we needed to get started if I wanted a family and a career."

She sips from her glass again and stares into the

night beyond the circle of light from the dim lanterns.

"He thought I'd change my mind once I had a baby. When I went back for my license when Jackson started preschool, everything fell apart. Arnold moved out, we split up, I got the job working for the medical group in one of their urban clinics. When the opportunity for this post came up, I felt called to take it. I thought it would be a good chance for us to start over."

"Well, you've been here a year. How do you feel about the ridge now?"

God knows I want her to tell me it feels like home for her. I want to hear her says she never wants to leave this pile of rocks I was raised on. Because I need her with me for the rest of my life and if she's planning on moving away there are hard choices that are going to need to be made.

Sage dips her head and I can see the curve of a sly smile on the corner of her mouth.

"It was a really good decision to come up here," she confesses. "Jax loves it here, he's got friends in school. He's got you..."

She turns to look up at me and her eyes shine in the moonlight with gratitude but I wish it was with the same desire I feel for her.

"What about you, Sage? You think you'll ever try again? Do you still want more kids?"

My glass is empty and so is hers. She takes them

both and hops off the swing, heading toward the house.

"I would *love* more kids," she tells me. "Jackson's always asking me for little brothers and sisters, but I'd have to meet the..."

She turns around and collides with my chest when she didn't realize I was right behind her. Hazel eyes find mine, her pupils blown out wide-- from sitting in the dark or from desire I'm desperate to see there, I'm not sure.

"...right man." She finishes her sentence on a breathless note that has my hands moving to cup her face.

Chapter Three

Sage

Rapid's lips burn against mine. Firm and commanding, he silently begs me to open for him. His tongue sweeps past my lips and claims my mouth with a heat I didn't think he felt for me.

His hand rests gently against the side of my face at first, but as our kiss deepens, it trails downward and brushes over my body.

The path his fingers takes leaves my skin sizzling in their wake. His other hand clutches my hip, pulling me against him so I can feel the thick ridge of his manhood as he presses it into my lower belly.

We bump up against the cabinets and for a moment I think he's going to lift me up and take me right here on the counter top.

My pussy weeps moisture in anticipation.

Taking advantage of my opportunity, I run my hands over his broad chest and down his torso, filling my hands with muscles sculpted from years of working outdoors on the river.

His thumb grazes my nipple and I arch my back and moan into his mouth while I pull the white tee he has under his flannel up so I can work my hands underneath.

I run my hands over his bare skin, and this time it's Rapid that moans between our kisses; but when my hands push lower to cup his hardness he pulls away with a tortured sound.

"Jax." He breathes harshly, my son's name barely a rasp in his thick voice.

"Sleeping," I remind him, reaching for him, desperate to feel him against me again.

Rapid's hands catch mine and bring them up between us. I can feel his heart beating hard and fast and both of us are breathing roughly. I don't understand why we're stopping. I don't want to stop but now he's pulling away when it seems obvious I'm not the only one who wants this.

"Sage, listen to me." He leans down so that he's eye to eye with me and I'm lost in the Mediterranean blue of his irises. "I want you, baby."

He takes one of my hands and presses it to his hard cock, pushing against me to let me feel his need for me. Thick, dusty lashes flutter over his eyes as they close and this time the furrow between his brows creases with an intense look of self-control as he takes my hand off him again.

"Then why--"

"Because Jackson is asleep in the other room. And he has no idea how I feel about you."

This time it's his hand that lowers, cupping my mound in a rough grip and pressing his fingers into me. I gasp and for a few, agonizing seconds, he tortures me with slow motions that have me grinding shamelessly against him.

"When I make you come for me, I'm going to have screaming my name till you lose your voice, understand?"

His grip on me tightens when he says it and everything inside me goes wet and hot with a reaction that is nothing less than primal.

"I've waited a whole year for you, Sage, I can hold out another few days. Jackson's going to be gone for a whole week and you better believe I plan on taking full advantage of that."

The smoldering look he gives has my clit throbbing. I don't know how I'm going hold out till Jackson's dad picks him up in a few days.

"Fuck," he curses under his breath and wraps me in his arms for another lingering kiss that sears my lips. "I need to get going."

Following him out to his truck, my body is begging me to convince him to stay but my brain knows he's right. Jackson doesn't know there's anything between us at all, it would be awkward to explain ourselves if he caught us doing anything he isn't expecting.

Outside, Rapid twists the key in the ignition and the big, diesel engine roars to life but he doesn't climb behind the wheel right away. Instead, he takes me in his arms with a vise-like grip and pushes me up against the side of his truck.

We're out of sight from the house, the neighbors, and anyone who might come up to the clinic's door after hours.

Rapid's body is pressed against mine without space between us, his hands are under my shirt, kneading my breasts with his mouth against my throat.

This time, when I reach to feel his rigid length filling my palm, he doesn't stop me. He presses into me and then grinds that hard pole against my mound when I reach for his perfect ass.

It's a frantic make-out session that has us both panting while our hands and mouths try to make up for a year's worth of lost time.

Rapid's hand dives under the fabric of my leggings and I'm so needy for him that I know I'll probably orgasm on the spot as soon as he touches me.

"Shit!" The unmistakable creak of our front door breaks the moment.

Rapid springs back from me.

"Mom?"

"Shit!" I echo Rapid's curse, quickly straightening my clothes and tucking my boobs back in my bra.

"I'm just saying good night to Rapid," I call back to the sleepy boy standing in the open door of the house. "I'll be right in."

"Night Rapid!" Jackson calls out to us. "Thanks for taking me camping."

"Any time, buddy," Rapid answers him. His voice still rough from arousal, he clears his throat and tells Jackson good night again and to have fun at the beach in a few days.

"Right," I nod, understanding, as Rapid gives me a stern glare that says both *"I told you so"* and *"I wasn't finished yet"* at the same time. "Okay, I'll see you in a few days then," I add, stepping back to a safe distance as he climbs into the cab.

"Damn straight you will," he says as he slips the truck in gear and backs out of the driveway.

Rapid

Pulling up to the doc's house, I go lift the toolbox and the bag of parts out of the bed before knocking on her door.

I know I told her I'd be back after Jackson's dad came to get him but it's been bugging me that her landlord hasn't sent maintenance up to repair that dishwasher.

And maybe I couldn't wait two more days to see her.

"Hey Rapid!" Jackson's voice greets me in tandem with the squeak of the door opening. I make a mental note to oil those hinges while I have the tool kit here.

"Hey bud," I hand the bag of parts I picked up from the hardware store to him as he leads me back into the house. "Your mom around?"

"She's working," he tells me, looking inside the bag and scrunching up his nose at the assortment of washers and plumber's tape inside. "What's all this?"

"I thought I'd fix the dishwasher for you guys."

Setting down my toolbox, I strip off my flannel shirt and drape it on the back of a kitchen chair before crawling under the sink to shut off the water valves and unplug the dishwasher.

"Cool. I hate doing dishes by hand," Jackson tells me.

I can't help but chuckle. I grew up in a house where my brothers and I took turns *being* the dishwasher, Jackson thinks doing dishes means stacking the machine.

"So, are you excited about seeing your dad?" I ask as I investigate the source of the problem. When

I'm met with silence I turn and look back to see Jackson standing nearby, working his lower lip in a thoughtful pout.

"What's wrong, bud?"

His thin shoulders lift and drop and he makes a face that's supposed to say *"no big deal"* but looks a lot like disappointment.

"Dad can't come," he tells me. "He said he has to work or something."

I'm glad I'm still part-way under the sink so he can't see the anger boiling inside me. Everything I know about Sage's ex tells me he's a loser that doesn't deserve a kid like Jax.

If you ask me, any man who breaks this many promises to his kid doesn't deserve kids at all.

"I'm sorry, man," I fight to keep the anger out of my face and give Jax a sympathetic look. "I know you were really looking forward to seeing him this week."

This time when Jackson shrugs there's no trace of covering up his real feelings.

"Eh, I don't really care about seeing my dad," he tells me honestly, "but I was really looking forward to going to the beach. I've never seen the ocean."

Even though it shouldn't, I'm relieved to hear it.

"You don't miss your dad?"

"Not really," Jackson sits on the kitchen floor next to where I'm sprawled out under the sink and I point toward the toolbox and ask him to hand me another wrench.

"I talk to him on the phone sometimes, but I haven't seen him since we moved here," Jackson volunteers, handing me the wrench I asked for.

I sit up so fast I konk my head on the cabinet before I clear it.

With a loud expletive that is definitely not the sort of thing I would normally say in front of Jackson, I hold my aching head with one hand and give him a hard look.

His eyes are round but we both bust out laughing.

"Do *not* tell you mother I said that word!" I warn him, even as the woman in question bursts through the door that leads to the clinic out front.

Chapter Four

Sage

A crash sounds from inside the house and I'm immediately worried about Jackson, until I hear the deep, male voice uttering a four-letter word that I definitely do not want Jackson repeating.

Fortunately, there aren't any patients in the clinic at the moment and I can leave the computer to go see what's going on.

When I get through the door that divides the clinic from the house, I find Rapid and Jackson on the kitchen floor laughing hysterically-- although Rapid is holding his hand to his head and there's a trickle of blood making its way out from under his hand.

"It wasn't me, Mom!"

"It was me," Rapid admits, "I'm sorry, I hit my head."

"Yeah, let me look."

"It's fine," he tells me, brushing my hands away when I try to get a closer look. "It looks worse than it is; you know how head wounds bleed," he says, getting to his feet and wetting a paper towel to hold against it.

"This, coming from the man who came to see me over a scratch that wouldn't have even made Jackson stop playing?"

The delicious looking man at my sink gives me a bashful grin.

"I might have had an ulterior motive for that," he confesses.

"Mom, can I go see if Cody's home?"

"Yeah, but if you're going to stay over there, text me and let me know where you are, okay?"

" 'Kay, see ya guys later, then." And just like that, he's out the door.

"What are you doing here?" I ask, finally managing to pry Rapid's hand off his wound so I can get a look at it. "I thought you weren't coming back for a few more days."

It really is just a nick. It's already stopped bleeding.

"I wanted to get this dishwasher fixed for you guys," he says, "and I thought I'd get to see Jax one more time before he left with his dad for the week..."

My face must show how I feel about that.

"Yeah, what the fuck's that about anyway?"

Rapid sounds pissed.

I just shake my head.

"Jax said he hasn't even seen his dad since you guys moved up here? I thought you said your ex made good money, getting out this way to see his son shouldn't be a hardship."

"It's not the money. Arnold didn't stick to the custody schedule even when we were in the same zip code. It's why I didn't have trouble moving Jackson out of state when I took this job. And since we moved up here, Arnold's promised at least five times that he's going to fly out to see Jackson.

"He never shows. It's always something."

"That's fucking bullshit, Sage," he mutters, dropping back down to crawl under the sink. "Men like that shouldn't be allowed to be fathers."

Pulling out the chair from the kitchen table that has Rapid's flannel shirt draped over it, I take a seat and admire the view.

Long, muscular legs stretch out across the tile of my kitchen floor, clad in faded blue jeans that fit loose at his waist. He's wearing a light blue t-shirt with his family's business logo on the front above a graphic of a Bigfoot paddling a kayak that says "Jonesing for the river" beneath it.

The shirt rides up as he raises his arms to work

on some part of the plumbing between the sink and the dishwasher.

Tanned skin stretches taut over abs made for licking, a trail of sandy colored hair a shade darker than his beard leads from his chest and disappears under the waistband of black briefs visible where the jeans have pulled low on his hips.

Is it weird that I'm actually hoping for a glimpse of plumber's crack?

This man *wants* me, I think, remembering the feel of his hardness pressed against me, the heat of his lips on mine. All the filthy things he promised to do to me as soon as we have a chance to be alone.

A heavy sigh escapes me.

"It'd be so much easier if Arnold would just sign off his parental rights altogether," I muse aloud. "That way if I ever get remarried, my new husband would be able to legally adopt Jackson."

"You want to get married again?" he asks from the depths of my kitchen sink cabinet.

"Someday, sure, but Jackson and I are a package deal and it's not like I'm ever going to find a guy who loves Jackson like you do."

As soon as it slips out of my mouth, I regret it and seeing Rapid's body go still confirms my mistake.

"Sage--"

"You know, I left some stuff open on the

computer that I need to get back to. If you need anything, I'll be out front."

Without giving him a chance to respond, I dash through the door to the clinic where I take a full minute to breathe and come to terms with the fact that I just fucked up my chance to get in that man's pants.

Rapid

Sage might think she said something to scare me off, but that couldn't be further from the truth. Hearing her say she'd like to get married again, and knowing that she sees how I feel about Jax? That has my heart beating double time as I try to tighten the fittings on the line I replaced without getting sloppy.

Now that I know we're on the same page, there's nothing left standing between me and my plans to make Sage mine.

Sliding out from under the sink, careful of my head this time, I drop tools back in the box and run the washer on an empty load to make sure it's not leaking anywhere.

Once I'm convinced it's safe to leave unattended, I head through the door to her office, taking care to be mindful of any patients that might be out front.

Looks like a slow day for the doc, the clinic is empty and I find her sitting at her desk in the small office, staring at the computer screen as the screen saver moves lazily across the monitor.

She's fucking gorgeous. Her hair is pinned in a loose knot like she usually wears it on her work days. My fingers itch to pull that clip and watch those dark locks fall free.

Her cheek rests against a loose fist, propped up by an elbow leaning on the desk beside the mouse. It forces her lips into a thick pout, her chin wrinkled in a way that makes her look irresistibly cute.

Today's uniform of forest green scrubs stretches over her full breasts and round hips yet still manages to hide most of her tempting figure.

Taking her all in from the partially open doorway, I let myself think of her as mine-- truly mine-- for the first time.

Knowing I'm not fighting an uphill battle against her past or her concern for her son or a career that could have taken her away from my mountain has me feeling bold.

Sage startles at the light knock against her office door and when she looks up and sees me, I know what she sees; a man obsessed.

"Rap--"

My name dies on her lips, drown in the kiss I'm laying on her as I pull her from her chair and wrap her in my arms.

The bell on the clinic door chimes, interrupting us before I can say a word.

Before Sage can get out the door of the office, the scurry of small feet running through the lobby makes its way to the hallway outside the door and the excited voices of young boys talking at once echoes off the walls.

"Whoa, whoa, whoa." Sage tries to calm Jackson and his friend down and get them to talk just one at a time while I hover over her shoulder.

"Can Jackson go to camp with me and Toni now?"

"Please, Mom? Please?"

Looking over Sage's shoulder, I see a Cody Yates standing shoulder to shoulder with Jackson, both boys giving Sage desperate puppy dog eyes.

"We talked about this, Jax," Sage says apologetically, "you were supposed to be with your dad this week."

"Yeah, but Mom, he's not coming. So now I can go to camp instead."

I let my hand slide down Sage's spine till I'm fingering the drawstring waistband of her pants. When she shivers at my touch, I know she knows what I'm thinking.

She turns around and gives me a look that silently begs me not to get Jax's hopes up.

"His plans fell through, doc," I say quietly, "why not let him go with his friends?"

"Pleeeeze." The boys beg in unison.

"The deadline for registration was two weeks ago," she explains to both me and the boys. "It's too late to get in now."

Eight-year-old faces fall and Cody's arm reaches around his buddy's shoulder in an already perfected bro half hug.

"I'm sorry, boys. If I'd known Jackson's dad wasn't coming, I'd have sent in the forms."

"It's OK Doctor Everett," Cody assures Sage.

"Yeah, Mom, I get it. Thanks anyway."

The boys leave through the clinic side of the house the way they came in, albeit much quieter.

Sage's shoulders droop as she watches them shuffle out the front door.

"I feel awful," she says without turning toward me. "He really wanted to go to that camp more than he wanted to see his dad. He was only excited about Arnold coming out because he was looking forward to the beach."

"This the miner's camp experience that Hart's Gulch hosts by any chance?"

Moonshine Ridge is home to a lot of camp outfits, both private and public, but the one that's most popular with the local kids is the week-long educational event that pays tribute to the ridge's mining camp roots. Any gold the kids find, they get to keep.

"Yeah," she says, "that's it. Apparently, it's *the*

social event of the summer for kids under twelve on the ridge. Jax was so disappointed he wasn't going to be able to go.

"I tried to talk Arnold into coming out a different week but he swore this was the only time he had available."

The sound that makes its way out of me is more of a growl than I intended, but this deadbeat dad routine is getting on my last nerve. If the loser ever does show up on the ridge, he's in for a hell of a man to man with yours truly and my fist.

"I know," Sage sighs and heads for the house with me close behind. "I really thought he'd make it this time. He had their whole week planned, he even sounded excited about it."

"Well, here's the good news," I take her by the shoulders and turn her to face me, "Mable Hart just happens to be my grandmother's best friend."

"Hart as in..."

"Hart's Gulch Gold Camp? That'd be her, yup. Vera even does most of the cooking for the camp every year. Teaches Dutch oven cooking for the older kids at the camp."

"I can't take advantage of your personal connections like that," Sage says, "that's not fair to other kids that couldn't go."

She stares at me openly while I laugh.

"Jax is in," I declare with a voice that says it's final. "There is not a kid on the ridge who wants to go that doesn't get to. Mable Hart doesn't leave anyone out. I'll let her know Jax will be on the bus tomorrow morning. All he needs is his sleeping bag and spare clothes and you can fill out the release forms online."

Chapter Five

Sage

Rapid Jones is officially my son's hero...and mine. He was able to talk to his grandmother and her friend that sponsors the mining camp and get Jackson registered at the last minute.

Then he met us at the school parking lot where the buses pick up and drop off the kids to say goodbye to Jackson and his little friends.

Jackson was so grateful that Rapid's connections got him into camp, he even forgot his usual manly cool handshake that they do and went straight for a hug.

He never did get a chance to finish whatever it was he came to my office to say yesterday, so I don't know what the situation between us is. I got the impression he's still interested in some alone adult time while Jax is at camp, but I need to keep any ideas about anything more than that out of my mind.

Rapid is great with Jax but that doesn't mean he's interested in signing on to raise another man's child. No matter how much better he is at than the sperm donor that can't even be bothered to keep a video call appointment.

When Rapid follows me back to my place after the buses leave, I'm a little confused and a lot turned on.

"What are you doing?" I ask, giggling like a teenager in front of her crush when he meets me at my door.

His hands are already on me, making me glad that the house's private entrance isn't visible from the street.

"It's nine in the morning," I tell him, not exactly trying to fend him off.

It always surprises me how soft his lips are; his skin is so darkly tanned and weather-worn, with the creases between his brows and at the corners of his eyes that prematurely age him in the sexiest of ways.

His beard brushes against my throat and his hands are already under the t-shirt I threw on to take Jax to the bus this morning.

"I was thinking you might be interested in a little sleep-away camp time too." Sapphire blue eyes sparkle with mischief, while his thumbs work small, firm circles over my pebbled nipples under my bra.

"Mmm," I moan and manage to get the door unlocked. We tumble through together and he pushes me against the wall just inside. "Paddling up river does not sound like my kind of weekend," I tease, arching my back and pressing into his touch.

"I was thinking my place." He whispers, his mouth on my neck, working its way down. "Up at Riverbend. My bed, on the river where the neighbors aren't going to call the sheriff when you start screaming."

"What makes you so sure I'll be the one doing the screaming?"

My hand slides over his broad chest and below the edge of his jeans. He's so hard already, and the swollen head of his cock can't be contained below the denim.

When I slip my hand under the elastic of his underwear, I get my first real sense of just how big he is. I mean, we were doing some pretty heavy dry humping against his truck the other night but now that I have him in my hand?

I'm a doctor, I went to medical school. I've delivered babies. I know how things work and I'm still not sure how I'll be able to take him. But damn am I going to enjoy trying.

"Because I'm more of a moaner than a screamer,"

Rapid jokes without pausing his journey toward my breasts.

He pulls my shirt over my head and unhooks my bra, letting it fall off my shoulders and drop to the floor between us.

When he bends to take one nipple in his mouth, I lose my grip on his length.

"Bed time," I say, pushing away from the wall with his mouth still on my breast.

"Those are doctor's orders I can follow."

Before I have a chance to take a step, Rapid's arms catch me under my back and knees, easily lifting me in a bridal carry position and hauling me to my bedroom.

Damn. I knew he was strong, but I'm not a featherweight and he just carried me as easily as he'd pick up Jax.

As soon as he lays me down on my bed, he grabs my hips and pulls me to the edge. My leggings are gone in one swift pull and Rapid's head is between my thighs.

I'm glad I showered this morning, not that I think it would have deterred this man if I hadn't.

"Fuck, baby, you have the prettiest pussy," he says in a voice that sounds like awe. "Relax, sweetheart, let me taste you."

This is the moment I get nervous. I haven't been with anyone but Jackson's dad since Jackson was born. Like I said, I'm a medical doctor, I've seen it all. I've reassured many a woman after a vaginal birth that everything down there is still intact but when it's me? Yeah, the thought crosses my mind that things might not be what this man expects.

"Sage." His voice is even deeper than usual, huskier, but soft and gentle as he kneels between my thighs and strokes through my soaking wet folds with a single digit. "I meant it, you're fucking gorgeous. Everywhere, baby. I've been dreaming of doing this since the first time I saw you--"

His hand runs up my inner thigh and then splays out over my stomach, his thumb rubbing lightly in soothing movements.

Raising up on my elbows, I gaze down to meet his eyes. I was nervous, feeling self-conscious of the bright sunlight spilling through the window at not even ten in the morning, of my curves and the stretch marks and a thousand other less than perfect things I could list about myself. I was worried that when I looked down at him, I'd see disappointment or regret in his face.

What I see is a man completely consumed by desire-- *for me*-- as he lowers his face and inhales my scent.

"Fuck woman," he says on a groan, "I knew you'd smell this good."

Then his eyes look up to mine and there's fire there. His hands grip my thighs and force them wide.

"This pussy's mine now, Sage," he tells me, the soft tone from before now hard with need, "I want you to come on my face and let the whole damn neighborhood know who you belong to."

My doubts are shattered with the first stroke of his tongue.

Rapid lives up to his promise, licking along my seam and suctioning over my clit while he slips a finger and then two inside me and begins moving them in time with the quick flicks of his tongue over my swollen bud.

I've never come so fast or so hard from oral before.

He keeps me on edge, teasing me till I'm begging for release and then he gives it to me. My thighs clench around his head and my hands fly over my mouth when I realize I am, indeed, screaming his name.

Rapid

Once Sage relaxes, her body gives in to the moment, responding to my attention without hesitation. Her pussy tastes like heaven, I want to eat this every morning. And I plan to.

I had no idea getting her off was going to be so easy, it's like she's on a hair trigger and all it takes is one more stroke against her g-spot while I suck her clit hard and she's screaming my name just like I told her to.

Her inner walls clench down on my fingers and I drink up every bit of cream she gives me while her hips buck so wild, I have to throw my other arm under her thigh and grab onto her ass to keep my mouth on her.

"You are fucking amazing when you come, doc." I lay a kiss to the inside of her trembling thigh, unable to resist nipping it and sucking till there's a tiny mark left behind.

Sage pants heavily, trying to catch her breath, watching me with lust-dazed eyes as I yank off my shirt and unbutton my jeans.

I can't wait another second. I have to get inside her or things are going to get messy real quick.

"Here, let me." She pulls herself up and reaches for my dick as soon as I have my clothes on the floor.

Her mouth is hot and wet as she slides those full lips of hers over the head of my throbbing cock.

I've dreamed of this a thousand times. Jerked myself off to the thought of what this would feel like and now that it's happening, I know my imagination did not do it justice.

Her hand wraps around the base of my shaft and gives it a firm stroke as her mouth slides down till I feel her throat constrict around my head.

Holy fucking hell, this woman is going to be the death of me right here and now, I think. It's a damn good thing she's a doctor because I think I'm about to have a heart attack.

"You gotta stop now," I command as I pull her off my dick before I explode in her mouth.

Laying her back, I follow, letting our bodies press together as I take her mouth with mine one more time.

"I need to come inside you." It's little more than a grunt as I work my way between her thighs with mine. "I want to feel you coming on my bare cock and I don't care if you're on birth control or not, Sage."

The tip of my dick is leaking precum and her pussy is soaking for me all over again. I take myself in my hand and draw through her silky lips. My dick jumps when her hips tilt to meet me.

"Rapid, I--"

"You're going to marry me," I tell her firmly, "You're going to be my wife and Jax is going to be my son and we're going to make a ton more babies together, so if that starts now, I don't care. You know I'm clean. I don't want anything between us."

"For fuck's sake, fuck me, Rapid!"

Her hands grab my hips with a strength I wouldn't have thought she was capable of as she pulls my aching cock into her needy little pussy.

The velvet smoothness of her tunnel has me

fighting to catch my breath as she takes me almost all the way to the hilt before she adjusts her hips beneath me.

"Shit, baby, you OK?" I freeze in place, worried we're going too fast.

Her pretty face is washed in lust; hooded eyes gaze up at me as she shakes her head against the pillows. "Give me more," she begs, tugging at me with her hands on my ass now.

She takes me all the way home, down to the root of my thick cock. So deep I have to stop and hold still for a count of ten before I can pull back and thrust in again.

This is insane. I've never felt anything like it before. I'm fighting not to blow my load like it's my first time. But damn if her body wasn't fucking made for me.

We're face to face; missionary style and I'm thinking about how she'd feel if I flipped her over and got her on her hands and knees but then she catches my lips with hers and I feel the tell-tale flutters of her pussy about to come.

It makes me speed up, thrusting harder and deeper. We're both covered in sweat and the sound of our bodies slapping together combined with hard breathing and grunts and moans fills the room with obscene music that's so fucking erotic I'm starting to wonder if I'm going to outlast her or not.

Then Sage comes for me. Her tight channel

squeezing so hard around my girth that I have no choice but to slam home one final time and empty my balls deep inside her, painting her womb with my seed.

Both of us are still shaking with the aftershocks of the simultaneous orgasm long after we've collapsed in each other's arms.

"Damn woman."

I want to tell her that I love her. Tell her that I knew more than just that I wanted her that night we showed up after hours. I knew she was mine. And the moment I met Jax, I knew he was mine too.

Dad always told us boys growing up that when you know, you know, but until I met Sage, I thought that was just a saying.

I want to tell her all the plans I have for us and I especially want to pack her a bag and get her up to my place where we can spend the rest of the week doing more of this in every position.

But Sage is already asleep with her head resting against my chest and I can't deny that a nap sounds like a good idea.

Chapter Six

Sage

After a week up at Rapid's house I feel like I'm walking on air. That is, when I can walk at all.

Driving back and forth to town for my scheduled shifts at the clinic haven't been too bad either and Rapid says the road between his place and town stays plowed all winter.

Yeah, he's been working hard to convince me to move in with him.

While Jackson has been at camp, we've done more than just make love on every available surface of both of our houses; we've also had far more serious discussions about our future together than our heat-of-the-moment declarations.

Rapid is all-in with making a family with me

and Jackson-- and any more additions that come along.

We just need to discuss it with Jackson.

Standing beside Rapid while we wait for the buses to bring the kids back down from Hart's Gulch, I can't help but feel nervous. I'm more worried about how Jackson will react to news of us getting married than I am about telling my parents.

I know Jackson has developed a special bond with Rapid, but that doesn't mean he'll be thrilled to learn that Rapid and I have our own special bond. Jax and I have never seriously discussed the possibility of me getting remarried.

It's been just us for a few years now and dating was never something I had interest in.

"You okay, babe?" Rapid whispers against my ear, leaning down to kiss me sweetly on the side of my face as the buses pull into the school parking lot.

When we spot Jackson getting off the second bus in line with his friends Cody and Toni, Rapid takes his arm off of my shoulders and shoves both hands in his pockets.

"Mom!" Jackson spots me and then sees Rapid with me. His little face breaks into a huge grin as he rushes toward us.

"Rapid." He slides to a stop in front of us and he and Rapid do their secret handshake thing.

My kid looks like he grew up by another three years in the week he was gone. I swear he's an inch taller and he's standing straighter, making his shoulders seem wider than I remember. He's sporting a tan, and from the peeling skin and lingering pinkness over his forehead, I can see that sunscreen wasn't his top priority.

"See ya at school, Jax." His friend, Toni says as she walks by, carrying a backpack toward waiting parents.

"Yeah, Toe, see ya."

Oh shit.

He's only eight for fuck's sake.

But neither me nor Rapid miss the blush that creeps into my son's face as he tries not to be obvious about watching the little girl that I thought was just another buddy while she waves goodbye from the back seat of the SUV.

Rapid pats him on the head and gives me a knowing grin.

"You wanna go bring the car around while I help Jax find his gear? We'll meet you right here in a few, okay--"

I forget about my growing boy mom worries and laugh as Rapid cuts himself off before finishing his sentence with what's become his usual "babe" pet name for me.

"You two behave," I warn, seeing a glint in Rapid's eye that lets me know he's up to something. "I'll be right back."

Jackson gives another boy a laid-back greeting

as the other boy says hi and also mentions meeting up again when school starts after the long weekend.

He's getting so big so fast.

As Rapid and Jackson head off toward the sidewalk where the bus drivers and chaperones are setting out all the luggage that they unload from the buses, I see them deep in conversation and all my worries about how Jackson is going to handle our news melt away.

Rapid

"So, what's up with you and Mom?" Jackson goes straight to the punch as soon as we've cleared Sage's earshot.

"Cody says you guys are into each other."

"Cody said that?" I wrack my brain to think of when Cody would have seen me with Sage.

"Yeah, he says we interrupted you guys making out when we came into the clinic the other day."

Oh. That's right. Whoops, thought we played that pretty cool.

Another girl says hi to Jackson as she passes by. She's a cutie, with long, twin pony tails and freckles but Jax waves nonchalantly at her without a sign of the blush that Toni got from him.

Making a mental note to open some conversations about girls in the not-too-distant future, I use the time to collect my own thoughts.

"So?" Jax turns his attention back to me as we make our way toward the jumble of backpacks, duffle bags, and small suitcases that have been stacked on the sidewalk.

"So what?" I return.

"Are you into my mom or not?"

Nothing gets by this kid, that's for sure.

"Well, that's what I wanted to talk to you about." I give him the straight answer he deserves. "While we have a minute, man to man."

Jackson pulls the youth backpack I got him for our paddling trip out of the pile and hoists it onto his shoulders with an ease he didn't have just a few weeks ago.

Moving aside, out of the fray, I kneel down so I'm eye to eye with Jackson while he gives me a stoic look.

"Would it be okay with you if I *was* into your mom?" I watch his reaction closely, looking for any sign that he's playing it cool when it isn't.

Instead, his face breaks into a big grin that reveals a new missing tooth. His fist pumps the air and I get an enthusiastic "Heck yeah!"

That has me laughing and feeling a whole lot better about my next question.

"Good, because here's the deal," I say seriously, "I

want to ask your mom to marry me. But I wanted to clear that with you first."

His head tilts thoughtfully.

"So, you'd be my dad?"

"Pretty much looks that way," I say.

"Are you guys going to have more kids?"

Before I can answer, Jackson rushes into a demand for "lots" of brothers and sisters, even though they'll be babies and cry a lot but he doesn't care because he's always wanted brothers and sisters and he thinks I'll be a great dad.

By the time we've hashed things out as men, and I've sworn Jackson to secrecy about our private conversation, Sage has the car pulled around and is waiting on us to get our butts in gear-- we promised Jax we'd take him out for burgers and shakes at the tavern in town.

That's when Sage is going to break the big news, but I already gave Jax the heads up and told him to play it cool.

Naturally, he does not.

He talks our ears off for the short ride to the tavern, telling us all about gold camp and his new friends and tells me my grandmother said to say hi.

Once we're situated in a booth and have burgers and shakes ordered along with a side order of the house specialty chili cheese fries with all the extras, Jackson pulls out a small vial from his pocket and proudly shows us the gold nugget he found while panning.

It's tiny, but it's still an impressive haul.

"Jackson," Sage says when the milkshakes have been delivered and Jax has settled in one place, "Rapid and I want to talk to you about something important."

"Yeah," he says, "Rapid already asked if he can marry you. I said yes."

"Way to keep it on the down-low there, bud." I can't help but laugh. He sounds so serious.

Sage turns toward me in the booth and smiles.

We've talked about our plans for the future, she knows my intentions.

"You asked Jax for his blessing?"

"Well, I had planned on this going differently," I admit as I reach into my pocket, "but since Jackson did, indeed, give me his blessing--"

I can't believe I'm doing this here, in Cedar McAllister's tavern of all places, on a busy Saturday afternoon in front of half of fucking Moonshine Ridge but...

Slipping back out of the booth I do the whole one knee thing and pop the velvet box open.

"Sage, will you do me the honor of--"

I don't get any further. Sage has her arms wrapped around my neck and her sweet lips pressed to mine so firmly I'm pretty sure I'm about to get eighty-sixed from the tavern for the second time in a year.

Pretty embarrassing after I had to grovel to Cedar to let me back in after Hayle skipped town.

"That's a 'yes' folks!" Millie, the day cook, bangs a spoon on a pan and shouts to the house, whether they were paying attention or not. "Now get out of the aisle, Jones."

Sage lets me slide back into the booth while I slip the ring on her finger.

"Are you guys going to be gross like that a lot?" Jackson asks, eyeing us suspiciously.

"Yeah," I answer honestly, "we are."

Epilogue 1
10 months later

Sage

Watching my men run down the beach, dragging a kite through the air, I can't help but feel emotional. Or maybe that's the hormones.

Rapid and I got married late last fall in a low-key courthouse ceremony in Slow River. Just me and him and Jackson, with a couple of court employees stepping in as witnesses.

We wanted to make it official quick and neither of us needed a big to-do. With two of Rapid's younger brothers also getting married this year, the Jones family has plenty of other weddings to coordinate.

Although, Rapid's mom and grandmother-- Annie and Vera-- have come up with a plan to throw one collective reception for all three couples later this summer.

The boys are ribbing their youngest brother, River, that he only has a couple of months left to find his own woman so he can get in on the party too.

Rapid's foot catches in the sand out on the beach and he goes down hard, kite falling into the surf as Jackson runs out to rescue it from getting pulled out to sea.

I sip my virgin colada. It's not quite the same without the rum, but it definitely suits the sunshine and salt spray off the Pacific ocean while I lounge in a camp chair and watch the boys have their fun.

As soon as Rapid and I knew for sure, we checked the calendar and started working on our plan for this trip.

The ocean is a lot closer to Moonshine Ridge than it was to our landlocked state back in the city, but it's still a solid eight hours by car. So, we decided to catch a flight out of Slow River's sleepy, rural airport into SeaTac where we rented a car.

Jackson has now seen the Pacific from three different states along our drive down the west coast from Seattle to where we'll eventually fly back home from San Diego.

Rapid and I agreed we'll break the big news tonight, over fish and chips on the dock in this touristy California beach town.

"Hey Mom," Jackson runs up and squishes me with a big hug and plants a kiss on my cheek. "Hey baby joey." He plants a second kiss on my growing bump.

He started calling the baby "joey" when we told him I was pregnant and it's stuck, even after we found out last month that we're having a little girl.

"Hey mama," Rapid joins us, drenched kite in hand, and gives me a kiss of a much different sort, reminding me that I'm six months pregnant and horny as hell. Something I'd heard from friends and patients, but certainly never experienced with Jax. But maybe it has more to do with my sexy husband than with the baby hormones.

"You two ready to clean up and get some dinner?" I ask, prying myself out of my chair with a little help from my hubby's strong arm.

Seriously, I'm not even that big yet, but getting in and out of these folding chairs is already a chore.

Rapid collapses the chair I was sitting on and adds it to the hand with the kite, snaking his other arm protectively around my shoulders and drawing me close.

He's shirtless, in a pair of board shorts and sport sandals, with acres of those delicious muscles on display under what seems to be permanently tanned skin. I lean in and inhale the scent of the salt and sand mingling with his natural smell and I know we're going to need to get creative to sneak some alone time once we get back to the room.

It's a strange conversation to have with your nine-year-old child; trying to explain to them that their birth parent happily gave up his rights as a father at the offer to get off the hook for any further child support payments.

Not that Arnold was paying much to begin with. Our incomes are close enough that if he'd held up to his end of the dual custody arrangement and actually taken Jax on a regular basis, he wouldn't have owed me anything. It was the fact that I have Jax full time that had the court ordering him to chip in.

When Jackson's dad found out that Rapid and I were engaged, he hit me with a legal suit to change the amount he owed me, saying that my new husband should be able to provide for me and my son now.

After Rapid was done telling Arnold exactly what a piece of shit he is, I counter offered to drop all future financial obligations of him if he'd sign off his rights-- and the jackass took the offer on the spot.

Jackson fixes me with a thoughtful stare and never stops chewing the battered cod strips from the basket in front of him the whole time I'm speaking.

When I finish, his eyes shift from me to Rapid and back before he wipes his hands on a napkin and reaches for his drink.

"Soooo..." he draws out slowly after setting the cup back on the table, "if Dad isn't my dad anymore..."

His glance darts quickly, almost shyly, back to Rapid before zeroing in on me again. There's a glimmer of hope in that quick glance that has emotion welling up inside me.

Rapid's hand slides from where it's been resting on my knee under the table a little higher and gives me a gentle squeeze when he hears my voice crack.

"Well bud, that's what we wanted to talk to you about," Rapid takes over for me while I grab a spare napkin and blink away the tears that have sprung up to my eyes.

His hand leaves my thigh and he drapes his arm around my shoulders, offering me silent support.

"How do you feel about letting me adopt you?"

This time Jackson's excitement isn't hidden. His eyebrows shoot up his forehead and his eyes go wide at Rapid's suggestion.

"Ohmygod! Can he, Mom? Can Rapid adopt me and be my dad for real now?"

Watching Jackson bounce in his seat with excitement at the prospect is enough to put me over the edge. Rapid's arm holds me tight as I break out in full blown tears.

"Mom? What's wrong?"

My son's voice as he rushes to my side only makes me cry harder. That protective tone he uses as he wraps his thin arms around me is one hundred percent Rapid's influence-- already teaching him how to be a man.

"I'm just happy, honey," I croak out.

"Girls are so weird," Jackson shakes his head at Rapid, but he doesn't loosen his arms around my neck.

Suddenly I'm laughing and crying, wiping the tears away while feeling loved and protected between my two favorite mountain men.

Epilogue 2
Five Years Later

Rapid

I keep a firm eye on Jackson and Toni as they paddle one of the tandem kayaks out on the calm water of the late season river.

When your son's best friend is a girl at eight is one thing; now that they're closing in on fourteen, it's a totally different ball game.

My brothers and their families are spread out all over the place, chasing kids, feeding kids, comforting kids who've scraped a knee or fallen in the water.

Current and Ginger's growing brood is with Cinnamon, over near the kitchen area, and I get the feeling that means one of my brothers is off somewhere making more kids.

"Things are lot different these days, aren't they?"

My buddy, Hayle, lays a cold beer in my hand and plops down on the chair beside me, using an opener on his key-chain to pry the top off one of the non-alcoholic root beers that Ginger bottles at her brewery in town.

"Amen to that," I answer, clinking my bottle to his without taking my eyes off the kids until I'm sure they're going to stick to the water for a while.

Then I let my gaze sweep across the family campsite till I find Sage. She's got things handled with the little ones, helping mom wrangle one of Eddy's boys into a life vest that he doesn't want to wear.

Man, I remember those days, being good enough at swimming that the vest seemed stupid while Vera and Don insisted I couldn't get in the boats without it.

Even my grandparents paddled down for this. They're getting up there in age now and they don't do the strenuous stuff anymore, but they weren't going to pass up an easy paddle downstream with a couple of great-grand kids in their boat.

"How the fuck did River get the voice, man?" Hayle points at my youngest brother, sitting beside the campfire with a guitar across his lap, singing a duet with Vera.

"Kid got all the talent," I say. The rest of us boys can't carry a tune in one of our drybags, but River can play about any instrument he picks up and sings like a damn angel. Just like our grandmother.

Pretty soon they've got a circle of kids sitting around them by the fire while they teach the kids to sing in a round.

Cinnamon's left the cooking to Mom and Current and she snuggles beside River with the baby on her lap, clapping his chubby little hands together to keep him from reaching for daddy's guitar strings.

"It's good to have you back, man." I turn toward the man beside me and give him a pat on the shoulder.

"Thanks man, good to be back," Hayle responds. If I didn't know the guy better, I'd think his voice sounded a little emotional. "Oh, that's me, man, gotta go." He jumps to his feet and heads toward the tent set up at the far edge of our site; leaving me to enjoy a few more moments of watching the family spread out around me till I hear mom call dinner.

A few of the older kids sprint for the grub line, Vera takes the plate that grandpa Don brings over for her and River and Cinnamon start singing an old John Prine song.

Then I see the best sight in the whole scene.

"Where's daddy?" I hear Sage's singsong voice as she leads our youngest in my direction. "Is that daddy?"

Landing's two and half-year-old squeal echoes

through the camp as he sees me holding out my arms for him a few feet away. I scoop my son up and hoist him into my arms before he has a chance to take a tumble in the dirt.

I also take advantage of the chance to catch my wife up in my other arm, pressing my lips to hers and savoring that feeling that still washes over me every time I have her near me.

"Where's Basil?" I ask, wondering which uncle or aunt our five-year-old daughter has persuaded into another tour of the river.

Grandpa Don took her on her first canoe ride when she was barely big enough to sit in his lap and she hasn't wanted to leave the river since.

"Your dad and Eddy have her and a couple of the other kids in the big raft." Sage tickles Landing's tummy and we head toward the food.

"Jax?" she asks.

"Right there," I nod toward our oldest who's carrying Toni's plate for her as they head for a seat by the fire.

Sage sighs heavily at the sight and I know how she feels.

A little while later, the whole family has found its way to the fire. River is strumming the guitar again while I help wipe Landing down from dinner.

Dad tries to tell us all the story about how he and mom got married on their first date-- again--

and Mom reminds him we've all heard it about a thousand times.

Oz and Meadow managed to make it down the mountain for a while. I see them across the circle with Hayle and January.

One of these days I need to stop by the tavern and thank Cedar for busting my buddy's nose a few years back. Funny how things work out.

Running to the Mountain

About
River Jones

Cinnamon says I'm off limits but she's the woman I've been waiting for.

Growing up, my brothers and I all heard the story of how Mom and Dad knew they were meant to be together the moment they saw each other. Somehow, I always knew that's how it was going to be for me too.

That's why I never took the opportunities I had to get more experience with any of the girls that came up to the river every summer.

Then I see Cinnamon; the cutie that got hired to help with camp support for the river rafting outfit my family owns.

One look at her honey-colored hair and the curves that have me dreaming of holding her close and I know I'm looking at my future in those sky-blue eyes of hers.

Too bad I'm her boss's son.

Cinnamon tells me she ran to the mountains looking for a fresh start, but we both know you can't run from fate.

Cinnamon

It's hard trying to start over when you haven't even started to begin with.

Not even twenty-one yet and I'm already trying to out-run my past. I can't afford to lose this job if I have any hope of getting the fresh start I desperately need.

River Jones is the handsomest man I've ever seen in my life, but the boss's son is strictly off limits.

Too bad no one seems to have explained that to him.

I'm doing my best to avoid getting too close to the tempting mountain man but when a sudden storm leaves me stranded with him overnight; there's just one tiny tent, just one sleeping bag, and just one need burning inside me.

Welcome to Moonshine Ridge and the rugged wilderness surrounding the remote mountain community where the history is long, the local lore is deep, and the men are as wild as the mountains they come from.

Protective, possessive, totally obsessed; the men of Moonshine Ridge will do anything necessary to claim the women they love and give her the happily ever after she deserves.

The Moonshine Ridge books contain a lot of insta-love, some swearing, some steamy scenes, zero cheating, and a lot of swoon-worthy happy endings. They're interconnected with recurring characters but can be read as stand-alones in any order.

Copyright © 2023 Rocklyn Ryder

All rights reserved worldwide
No part of this book may be reproduced, uploaded to the Internet, or copied without permission from the author. The author respectfully asks that you please support artistic expression and help promote anti-piracy efforts by purchasing a copy of this book at the authorized online outlets.

This is a work of fiction intended for mature audiences only. Names, characters, places, and incidents either are the product of the author's imagination or are used fictitiously. Any resemblance to events, locales, business establishments, or actual persons, living or dead, events, or locales is purely coincidental.

Chapter One

Cinnamon

When I came to Moonshine Ridge to work for the Jones River Expeditions, this wasn't exactly what I had pictured.

I knew I'd be part of the camp kitchen crew-- I just didn't realize that "camp" actually meant we'd be camping.

"You'll get used to the timing," Vera tells me, "you just have to remember half as many on top as on the bottom."

She's in her eighties and she looks like she fell asleep in 1967 and woke up this morning. Long, silver hair hangs in a single braid down her back with two feathers hanging from a thin. leather cord clipped in behind her ear.

In the few weeks that I've known Vera, I've

never seen her wear makeup and I'm not sure she owns a bra either. In the tie-dye version of the company's "Jonesing for the River" t-shirt, jeans, and hiking boots, Vera Jones embodies the essence of "mountain mama," with her tall, athletic build, even at her age, and the creases lining her face that tell a story of decades of life well-lived.

She's everything I'd love to become someday. Well, except for the bra part.

Today, she's teaching me how to calculate the number of charcoal briquettes I need for each Dutch Oven.

I thought the camp kitchen would be a permanent structure. A real mess hall with electricity and hot water on demand or at least one of those big, circus-sized wall tents with real kitchen equipment set up inside.

Instead, I'm learning how to cook everything from chili to peach cobbler over an open fire or in the big Dutch ovens with charcoal briquettes. Outside.

We-- me, Don, and Vera-- are support for the outfit. We haul all the gear for the multi-day expeditions from camp location to camp location in the bus; setting up the kitchen, cooking the meals for however many people are on the trip, cleaning up, tearing down, packing and heading to the next location to have it all set up again before the rafts make it down river to unload dozens of hungry rafters into camp.

It's a far cry from the restaurant job I had in the city before everything went to hell, and it might not be what I was hoping for when I sent out applications, but it's the job I was offered.

And cooking for a crowd of tired, sunburned, hungry campers on week-long river-rafting trips turns out to be a lot more fun than I thought it would be.

Hard, hot work, but fun.

Speaking of hot...

The arrival of our campers is preceded by loud voices echoing off the granite peaks that rise up on both sides of the river valley around us. Some of the voices are triumphant; whoops of victory for arriving in camp safely. Some are merely relieved; the people who tumbled out of the raft over the rougher stretches of rapids, the ones who forgot their sunblock, or are just sore and tired and starving and looking forward to hot food and a cot to crash in.

I look up from the prep table where I've been putting together the fixings to go with the burgers that Don's grilling over a bed of coals.

The first raft that pulls ashore is led by Rapid. He's the oldest of Bank and Annie's four boys and he got married recently.

In fact, all the Jones boys got married recently,

according to Vera. "Fell like dominoes this last year," she said.

All except--

No. The next raft is Bank's. In his fifties, Bank Jones still has a way to go before he hits official "silver fox" level, but he's close. With sandy blonde hair long enough to keep pulled back in a short pony tail and a beard that's streaked with gray, Bank Jones is just as lean and muscular as his sons.

Annie's raft comes in right behind her husband's.

From what I understand, she and Bank have been married for thirty-seven years. They got married on their first date. Which was a blind one, set up by one of Vera's friends. Bank tells the story every chance he gets.

I've heard a few people say they think it was a stupid move, but I think it's romantic. I love the idea of love at first sight. I love seeing a couple that it worked out for-- Bank and Annie are obviously still in love. As are Don and Vera, even after sixty years together.

The last raft pulls to shore.

My heart beats triple time as the pilot up front digs his oar into the sandy river bottom and calls out commands to the other paddlers in the boat, directing them so they keep the raft from making its way any further downstream while he jumps off the bow and into waist deep water.

Running to the Mountain

The late afternoon sun glistens gold on his tanned skin, reflecting off the droplets of sweat and river water clinging to the muscles of his arms, swollen from paddling a raft filled with twelve people down a river full of class three rapids all day.

As he grabs the handle at the front of the raft, I watch those muscles flex against the weight as he pulls the boat onto the sand and holds it while the passengers debark.

Then he yanks the empty raft farther on shore to keep it from getting swept away overnight, and then-- my favorite part-- he drops his paddle in the boat and unclips the buckles of his life vest. He lets it slip off his shoulders and drops it in the raft with his paddle.

And now I'm looking at River Jones in all his glory. Bare chest and thick legs, corded muscle, and a pair of sopping wet board shorts that are a far better sight than any pair of gray sweatpants could ever be.

He bends at the waist, drops his head forward and shakes like a dog. Blonde hair goes flying, water droplets scattering off him and I see it like it's in slow motion, before he stands back up and flips his wet hair back off his face in a graceful move.

Oh shit. Was that me? Did I just whimper?

"Careful, Don keeps those knives sharp," Vera says from behind me, "did you cut yourself? I'll get the first aid kit."

Nothing in Vera's first aid kit is going to help me though.

The only ache I have isn't going to be cured with a couple of aspirin.

River

"See something you like?"

Rapid tosses a towel over my head and punches me in the arm.

He's been razzing me about being the last one of us boys left single ever since he put a ring on Doc's finger last fall.

"Don't worry, we'll still let you into the party," he tells me while I pull on one of the company tees.

Our parents are throwing a big reception for my brothers and their wives at the end of the river season this year. Since every one of the assholes got married in a minute without letting Mom enjoy a proper wedding.

The guys have all been giving me hell, saying that I only have three more months to find a wife or I'm going to have to sit by myself at the party.

They don't bother me though. I grew up with three older brothers and I don't let them get to me. I know I can count on them for anything I need, just like mom and dad and Don and Vera. Family's the best and mine's better than most.

Besides, if I have things my way, this damn group reception is going to have two more plates at the couples' table; because my big brother is right-- I *do* see something I like.

Her name's Cinnamon. She's the girl Mom and Dad hired to fill in the gap in the kitchen support since Current left the guide company to open up the Brick and Porter brew pub and pizza joint in town with his wife, Ginger.

She's got eyes the color of the summer skies over the mountains; thick, honey-colored curls; and curves that make it impossible not to notice she's a woman. And ever since she showed up back in May to learn the ropes, noticing that she's a woman is about all I-- and my dick-- have been able to do.

"Seriously man, when are you going to do something about that?" Rapid chides with a chin-wag toward the beauty at the mess set up.

I make sure the edge of the towel is hanging low enough to save me from the embarrassment of whatever hell my oldest brother might put me through if he noticed the tent in my shorts.

Fuck me, man. Even the river's ice-cold, early season water can't keep my dick from misbehaving when I'm looking at Cinnamon.

"Do something about what?" I ask him, as he walks with me toward camp.

"Your crush on the new girl," he elbows me in the side as we get to the tent that's been set up for us to share while we're in camp overnight.

I shoot him a glare as he ducks under the flap before me. He catches it when he moves aside to let me in. The look on my face must give away more than an ill-timed chub ever could, because the dumb grin on Rapid's face falls right the fuck off.

"Oh." He whistles long and low. "Got it, man."

"Yeah, how was it that it took you over a year to make a move on the Doc?" I shoot at him as I yank my sleeping bag out of the duffle that's been tossed in the tent so I can set up for the night.

"That's a whole different situation, man," he answers as he gets his bed set up as well. "I had Jax to think about."

Jackson is Rapid's step-son now. Rapid's in the process of legally adopting him though so that's cool as fuck.

"Ask her out." Rapid tells me as he pulls a dry shirt over his head and flops back on top of his sleeping bag.

"What if she says 'no?' "

Rap snorts. "She can't say no, you're the boss's kid. She has to kiss your ass if she wants her job, right?

"Dude, you are so fucked up. That's like the actual definition of harassment."

Rapid drops an arm over his eyes and shrugs.

"Wouldn't know, I never messed around with any of the employees."

He's right. My brothers all spent their free time in camp entertaining the college girls that came up to spend summer break on the river.

Swapping my board shorts for some jeans and a dry shirt, I rummage through my bag and pull on my camp shoes.

After giving Rapid some shit about being an old man-- seriously, the dude's already half asleep and Don hasn't even gotten the camp fire stoked up yet-- I climb out of the tent and head toward the mess tent. Following the sweet smell of Cinnamon that's so strong, you'd think they already had the cobbler going.

But it's not cobbler and this tempting scent is mine and mine alone.

Chapter Two

Cinnamon

After convincing Vera I didn't cut myself, she went back to where the coals are ready to start baking the peach and berry cobblers that Vera prepared while I've been busy prepping and putting out the fixings for the burgers.

Don has hamburger patties coming off the grill and our hungry campers are starting to mill about the kitchen area in anticipation.

"Hey."

The voice behind me is deep and masculine. The single word rolls through me like approaching thunder and I thank my lucky stars he can't see my face as I try to compose myself before turning around.

There's only one man that voice belongs to and my body reacts to it like one of Pavlov's dogs to a bell.

Yes, parts of me are drooling. It's so embarrassing. I always thought it was an exaggeration whenever I heard one of my friends make a crude remark about her panties getting wet when she saw a guy she was crushing on, or when I read it in books.

I guess I just hadn't been crushing on the right guys.

Which is probably one of the reasons I never bothered fooling around with any of the guys I went out with before-- well, before I didn't have a chance to fool around at all.

Desperately wishing I was wearing a bra with more padding to hide my hardened nipples, I turn to face River and give him my best casual grin. The one that says I'm totally used to being around sizzling hot guys and he's just another co-worker.

"Hey, River." I'm so proud of myself, I don't stutter over his name or go all breathy and doe-eyed. "What can I get ya?"

Me. I think hopelessly. *Me; in your tent, in the river, spread out right here on the folding kitchen prep table with all the clients and your family eating hamburgers six feet away.*

Of course. That's not going to happen. It can't.

River Jones is my boss's son. Strictly off-limits.

Bank and Annie were so kind to hire me even

with my full disclosure of the record that's kept me from finding work. They've welcomed me without judgment and treated me like family. I'm relying on them for their reference so I can get a permanent job at the end of the summer.

I can't risk that for a fling with their son.

"Was thinking maybe you wanted to go for a walk later?"

His eyes are a gray blue with streaks of warm, hazel brown near the centers that change to a dark stormy hue as he stares back at me.

There's a pulse between my thighs begging me to go for that walk.

"Sorry, I can't," I mumble quickly, pulling my eyes away from his commanding stare and finding something to do to make myself look busier than I really am. "We have the clean-up and everything, you know," I add, as if I need an excuse to dodge his invite.

It's really more to convince me than him though.

"I've been coming on these over-nighters since I was born, I know there's plenty of time after everything's cleaned up and put away for support to sit around the fire with everyone. Or get away from everyone."

His voice has a lilt to it that makes my tummy do somersaults. Something dark around the edges of his usual bright tone that makes no mystery of what he means. River Jones is flirting with me. I'm sure of it.

I bet he knows exactly how much time there is after clean up. I bet he knows exactly where two people who want to get away from the after-dinner campfire gatherings can go.

The Jones brothers are all smoking hot. I've met Eddy and Current, the two that no longer work for the rafting business now they've gotten married and opened businesses of their own, and the oldest, Rapid, still works with the outfit.

It must have been surreal when all four of them were working as guides for the company.

And I'm sure every one of them had plenty of experience growing up like this-- working all summer getting tanned and jacked from swimming and paddling. I can't imagine it's hard to get laid when you look like that.

Throw in a bunch of horny college girls on vacation from the city looking for a good story to go home with and you've got the makings of every guy's dream job.

No wonder he's looking at me now like he's so sure I'm going go with him.

Knowing River's probably some cocky playboy that's had six different girlfriends every summer since he was a teenager should be enough to add some ice to the blood boiling in my veins, but it doesn't. Instead, my curiosity is piqued.

I wonder what this mountain man could teach me; and the way River's looking at me right now has me wishing I was just another college girl, that this was just another summer job, and that I could afford to risk having a fling with the boss's son.

River

"No really," she tells me from behind the lid of one of the big ice chests where she's ducked down to rearrange heads of lettuce, "I can't. I have to stay and help your grandparents."

Every time I've talked to Cinnamon, she's found a way to put something between us: Cars. Rafts. Oars. Lanterns. Lettuce.

She might be shy, but when I do manage to make eye contact with her, I know she feels it too. This pull toward each other.

I just don't understand why she keeps resisting it, it's almost like she's hiding something.

There's nothing she could tell me that would change how I feel about her though.

I grew up hearing the story about how Mom and Dad got married on their first-- blind-- date. Dad says he knew Mom was the one the moment he laid eyes on her and I always knew it was going to be the same way for me.

I was right. Cinnamon's my woman. I knew it the day she showed up and I'm not going to let her get away. She needs to understand that I'm not just looking for a hookup, I plan on making her mine forever.

"I'll see you at the campfire then," I tell her. I can't help but grin at the way she blushes as she ducks across the kitchen set-up to intercept Vera who's pulling the big Dutch ovens off the coals.

"Maybe," Cinnamon tells me as she uses the claw to pull the heavy lid off one of the Ductchies. Steam escapes and the smell of cobbler fills the air.

"Are you bothering my assistant?" Vera scolds when she sees me hovering.

My grandmother shoos at me to back up a few steps to give her and Don space to bring the ovens up to the table so they can start dishing out desert.

"I was just trying to convince her to come join the fire ring after clean up," I answer.

Vera glances back at Cinnamon, who's dishing out cobbler into bowls and ignoring me completely. Then she hands me a bowl and a spoon and gives me the look she's been giving me since I was a baby, the one that says I'm not fooling her.

"We'll all be at the fire once we get things cleared and ready for breakfast," she tells me, giving me a push to get me out of the way. "Go on and get that guitar warmed up, we'll be there in a jiff."

A few minutes later, I'm sitting on one of the log

benches that have been positioned around the fire ring at this site since before I was born. My cobbler is long gone and I'm strumming the old hand-me-down Taylor that Vera gave me when she realized I could play the thing.

My attention's on the kitchen crew though. Well, just one person, really.

Make that two.

This group of rafters has been rowdy. It's a corporate retreat type outing full of city folks out here playing adventurers.

Too many dudes trying to impress not enough ladies, and I do not like the way this one guy has been looking at my girl since night one.

Across camp, I can see Cinnamon dodging his attempts to corner her.

Don and Vera have already gone back to their bus to change into comfortable campfire clothes, leaving my girl on her own with whatever last-minute chores she's finishing up.

I can read her body language from here.

It's not the shy way she is when she's trying to hide her reaction to me. There are no mixed signals at all in the way she's side stepping the asshole who keeps trying to get in her space.

Handing the guitar over to Rapid so I don't break it over some asshole's head, I head over and put myself between Cinnamon and the idiot that can't read his audience.

"She's not interested, man." My voice doesn't even sound like me, coming out low and mean as my fists ball at my sides.

I'd like to swing right for that pitiful patch of scruff under his chin he calls a beard, but I've been working for the rafting business since I was old enough to be added to the payroll. This isn't the first idiot that's been on one of our tours, he won't be the last, and I know better than to punch a client.

I'm not letting him know that though.

"Sorry man, I didn't know she was taken." Scruffy McCity-Slicker cowers in front of me. "You could have just said you were with one of the guides, you didn't have to him come over to threaten me."

The guy scampers off, back to his buddies and Cinnamon gives me an unreadable look.

"Thanks, I guess," she tells me.

"You guess?" I tease.

"Well now they're all going to think we're a couple." She sounds sad about it, but I can't help but puff up with pride. I don't just like the idea that they're going to leave her alone now, I like the idea that they're going to think she's mine.

"So let 'em," I tell her, stepping into her space.

She backs up till her curvy ass hits the big, metal prep table that's been cleared and washed down for the night, but she doesn't try to duck me as I follow her till there's barely space between us.

Her big blue eyes are looking up at me as she shakes her head back and forth.

Off in the background, I hear the chords of one of Don and Vera's go-to campfire songs and I know my grandmother has taken over the guitar.

My hand itches to touch Cinnamon. Just to Smooth the curl that's sprung free of the wide headband she's wearing. Just that would be enough, I lie to myself as I reach toward her.

"River! Where'd you go? We need you over here before your dad starts singing!"

Mom's voice calls through the darkness, loud and full of laughter like it always is.

It's an established fact that Vera and I are the only ones in the family that can carry a tune, but genetic tone deafness doesn't stop Dad or any of my brothers from trying.

"You better go." Cinnamon's voice is soft, filled with air, and sounds as shaky as my hands feel. "I've heard your dad sing. Your clients will ask for refunds."

"Come on." The spell is broken but my cock is still painfully hard behind the zipper of my old jeans. "Let that idiot think you're mine. At least it'll keep him from bothering you again."

She lets me take her hand in mine and follows me willingly back to the fire.

When she moves in close to sit beside me on the old log bench, I give a smug grin to the guy staring daggers at me while I take the guitar that Vera's passing over to me.

I don't miss the knowing look on Rapid's face either, as he watches me position the guitar across my knee so that Cinnamon doesn't need to move farther away.

Chapter Three

Cinnamon

It's hard not to get caught up in the activities after our work is done for the day. There's always a campfire, usually hot chocolate and sometimes s'mores, while Vera and River take turns passing the guitar back and forth and singing mostly old folk music from Vera and Don's days as free-wheeling hippies touring America in their converted school bus back in the sixties.

Sometimes they sing something that the clients know and it becomes a big sing-along.

Tonight, I feel more like I've stumbled into the fire and not just sitting near it. Because I'm sitting way too close to River, our thighs touching while he holds the guitar so that it doesn't get between us.

When I try to move even slightly to give him

more room play, he gives me a possessive glare that tells me he's not OK with that. He slides a few inches over the old log bench that's been worn smooth by years of use and this time I don't move away when I feel the heat of his body against mine.

I sit quietly and suffer in silence, my body waking up at his presence. It feels like we're being pulled toward each other and it's getting harder to resist my urge to give in to my growing need for him.

No matter how bad I want to though, I can't let River distract me. Even when he's glancing toward me as he strums the instrument in his lap, looking at me like I belong to him.

River has nothing to lose here. He's family. He'll take over this business when his parents retire someday. He doesn't have to worry about anything, he's got people he can count on to always have his back.

This might be just another summer for him and I'm just the fresh meat at the market. A conquest to tick off his list and, to be honest, if I'd met him two years ago, when I had just turned eighteen and I thought my future was wide open in front of me? I'd have probably jumped on the chance for a summer romance with this Adonis.

But I can't now. I can't take any chances. Including a broken heart, because when River's long, nimble fingers bend the strings of the guitar into a familiar melody, I can't help singing along to the old tune.

I don't even know if anyone else is still singing with us. I only see River as he turns toward me and holds my eyes with his as we sing together and it feels so right.

It's just an old song. One my grandmother used to play when I was very little. The lyrics aren't meant for us and I remind myself that River singing them with me doesn't mean he's saying it for real.

When we finish the song, he moves immediately into another duet, a campy old seventies song that several of the group knows. Which is good, because I don't know all the words to this one and having so many other voices joining us lightens the mood, breaking River's intense stare off of me and giving me a chance to breathe.

One of the women from the group we're leading calls out a request for a country classic and River's fingers move over the strings, easily transitioning into the new melody. He leans into me again and Vera's voice joins in to support the lyrics that the woman doesn't remember.

Annie comes around, handing out long skewers and passing a bag of marshmallows. I watch Rapid hold his in the fire till it's a flaming torch at the end of his skewer while I carefully hold mine above the flames.

"Let me show you," River sets the guitar aside

and takes my skewer from me. For a second, my hand is enveloped in his. I can feel his callused skin against mine and there's no stopping my imagination from going straight to what those hands of his would feel like running over my body.

River stares at his older brother and shakes his head in disgust. "You seriously need to learn how to roast a marshmallow, bro," he tells him.

I watch River hold the skewer he took from me carefully above the edge of the fire where the coals are just a bed of glowing red.

"You have to be patient," he tells me softly. "You can't rush it."

Annie brings me another skewer, already loaded with a marshmallow, and grins at me as her eyes flick over to her youngest son, letting me know I'm in for a long wait if I let River be in charge of the toasting.

Campfires were not part of my childhood. I'd never cooked anything over a campfire till I took this job, let alone toasted marshmallows or made s'mores.

Mom and I lived in the city, in an apartment. It wasn't in the best neighborhood and it needed the carpet replaced about ten years before I was born, but it was a two bedroom.

Grandma lived a few blocks away and she was my babysitter till Mom met Jimmy. Jimmy took good care of us. Mom didn't have to work anymore and we moved to a nicer part of town to live in a real house.

When Mom and Jimmy bought land on the other side of the state, I moved in with Nana so I could finish high school with my friends.

River's hand on mine again yanks me out of my thoughts.

He turns my hand so that my marshmallow can toast on the other side, showing me how to keep it the right distance from the fire.

Someone should record him doing this, he's like some sort of Zen master of marshmallows.

He uses a graham cracker and a square of chocolate to coax the blistered sugar off the end of his skewer and hands the sticky treat to me, taking over the marshmallow I've been trying to work on just as diligently.

When his finger slips across the corner of my mouth to wipe away a bit of gooey marshmallow that went astray, my breath goes still and my heart hammers and when he slides the tip of his thumb between my lips, I know there's no way I'm going to make it through the summer without another taste of this man.

River

. . .

"What the fuck, man?"

I grumble from under the edge of my sleeping bag when I'm jarred awake with a rough kick to my feet.

"No time for your sleeping beauty act." My brother's voice teases as he kicks my feet again. "We got a change of plans for the day, weather's heading our way. Get up."

When I poke my head out and pry an eye open, I can see that it's later than I usually sleep when I'm outdoors.

Probably because I didn't get any fucking sleep all night. My dick was so hard I couldn't get comfortable. Even after sneaking out for a walk and jacking off, I was rock hard again by the time I got back in the tent.

I throw my arm over my eyes and groan. I'm still hard.

Last night with Cinnamon was amazing. It felt right having her beside me; singing together and showing her how to properly roast a marshmallow-- I can't imagine growing up without ever roasting marshmallows on an open fire-- but I can still feel her soft lips against my thumb when I swiped the melted sugar off the corner of her lip.

I've never been so turned on in my damn life. Just that much of her was enough to keep me awake nearly all night with a hard-on that won't fucking quit.

Rapid yells at me from the other side of the canvas wall beside me and I tell him to fuck off, but I'm already pulling on my clothes and my shoes.

This happens at least a couple times a season; summer storms roll up the river valley and rage against the mountains. Rain doesn't stop us, but it's not safe to be on the water when the thunderheads are involved.

The alert must be pretty serious if we're changing plans for the day.

When I emerge from the tent and make my way to the mess for breakfast, the group is unusually subdued, talking in low tones around the morning fire while clutching steaming mugs of coffee.

Rapid and my parents are holding a huddle with Don over by the bus that Don and Vera use as a camper that also transports all the camp gear from site to site. I'm about to head their way to get caught up on the plan but then I see her.

She's leaning against the last prep table that hasn't already been torn down and stashed on the bus. Most of the kitchen has been dismantled already, something that normally doesn't happen till the rafts are back in the water for the day.

I've been working the family rafting gig in one way or another since I was a kid. I know this drill; they'll be holding back in camp for a couple of hours later than usual and then they'll split the crew between vehicles and truck the clients to the next campsite.

The sun is out and the sky is still blue overhead, which means one of us will be going solo with a raft, taking basic supplies down river so the group arrives to hot drinks and a fire already going.

Since time is an issue, that'll be either me or Rapid. Rapid's faster on solo runs, so I'm in no rush as I fill a mug with coffee from the old pot that's still simmering on the camp stove.

"Honey." I say out loud as the sun glints off Cinnamon's hair. She's got it pulled back in a loose pony tail that still shows the natural curls and it shines a warm deep amber where ever curls have escaped to frame her face.

"No one's here," she tells me shyly. "You don't have to act like we're together."

Something about the blush coloring her cheeks and running down to the ample cleavage revealed by the company's V-neck t-shirt she's wearing tells me she doesn't really want me to stop.

Still. It wasn't what I meant.

"Your hair." I gesture toward her with the mug in my hand, "It's the same color as honey."

I'd been trying to figure out what her golden-brown curls reminded me of. Why my mouth waters every time I see them flying in the breeze. Or maybe it's not the honey-hued locks. Maybe it's the sweet face they frame, the feminine curves they accompany.

"My hair is hardly the color of honey." She blushes harder even as she snorts along with her sarcastic denial.

Pulling my phone of out my pocket and picking up the glass jar of local honey from the table beside the coffee pot, I step up close to her. Close enough to fill my lungs with her scent; the perfume of that dry shampoo she uses when she doesn't get a chance to wash her hair properly, smoke from the campfires that permeates every porous surface of camp all summer, fresh coffee that she must have ground this morning, and a musk that's entirely feminine and uniquely hers that pulls my dick back to attention faster than I can snap the picture.

We're close-- face to face-- and I'm playing with fire. Temping myself, pushing the limits of my own self-control because I'm a fucking glutton for punishment.

Or because it's worth it to watch the way she looks up at me with her pupils blown out wide, making her azure eyes look like the twilight sky after sunset. It's worth torturing myself like this just to see the way those spectacular tits rise and fall faster when I'm in her space.

Everyone's busy somewhere else right now. I've got Cinnamon all to myself and I'm thinking about how badly I need to taste those bee-stung lips of hers.

I move in, closing another few inches of the space between us. Leaning forward slightly, I set the jar of honey back on the table beside her hip, letting my hand trail along the curve of her ass where it's pressed to the edge of the table behind her.

It's not the first time I've tried to get close to her, but it's the closest she's ever let me get.

"Honey, see?" I hold the phone up with my free hand to show her the picture. Her hair shining in the morning sun, the same color as the wild-flower honey we get locally from Zephyr Hart's farm.

"River!"

Dad's voice growing closer as he hails me breaks the moment and sends Cinnamon flying to the other side of the of the table where she starts wiping down syrup bottles from the morning's pancakes and putting things away in the big crates to get them ready for transport.

"Oh! Cinnamon, good, you're here too. So, here's the deal, you two are going to take the raft down so the fire will be started and we'll have the basics ready for everyone when we get into the camp this afternoon. Got it?

"River knows the drill. We're looking at about a three-hour window before the storm reaches us. Don and Rapid already have the raft loaded up with what you'll need so you two need to get a move on.

We're gonna hang back with the group while Vera and Rapid head down, Eddy's coming up to help set up the shelter so people aren't stuck on the buses waiting. OK? Great, see ya guys later today."

The look on Cin's face while my dad spells out the plan is pure panic. I can tell she's not excited about getting voluntold into this, but Mom's already brought over a life vest for her.

There's no arguing when we're racing weather.

"Sorry honey, looks like we're going for a boat ride." I shoot her a wink but I'm thrilled that I get her all to myself for a while.

Chapter Four

Cinnamon

Thank goodness I have my own tent. I had my hands in my pajamas, desperately trying to relieve my aching clit more than once last night.

It's more than just how badly I want to River's body moving with mine, touching me in ways that no man has ever touched me before.

I can picture this being my whole life; just me and River, his wonderful family, the mountains and the river with me handling the kitchen while he handles the rafting. A cabin with a fireplace and a bunch of muddy children together.

But I woke up this morning determined not to get carried away with my fantasies. I know how easily plans for the future can dry up and crumble to dust. It's going to be a long time before I'm going to be able to live like a normal person without the stigma of a felony hanging over me.

It's best to stay away from this man-- the man who is cinching straps and buckling me into a life vest right now.

The man who was dangerously close to kissing me before I got called back to my senses and this crazy plan got thrown at me.

"Hey," he says, pulling my face up to his with a finger below my chin, "nothing to worry about. We do this all the time. It'll take two hours, max, for me to get us to the next site. I get the fire going, you heat water and get coffee going. Eddy's coming to meet up with us so they can get the big shelter up and then it's standard procedure from there. People get bussed down. Don and Vera bring down the support bus. You cook in the rain. Tons of fun."

"Fun." I echo numbly.

His mouth stretches into a grin that's nothing short of mesmerizing.

"Fun," he promises.

OK. I'm not the strongest swimmer, but I've got a life jacket on, and River is with me. I know he'd never let anything happen to me.

He sits me on one of the benches in the raft and shows me where I can hang on to a plastic handle for dear life, even though we're still on shore.

"It's not a white-water ride, honey," he smiles

when he says it but there's a concerned look in those storm blue eyes of his.

"Isn't that what you guys do?"

"Not every section has rough water," he explains as he checks to make sure that all the gear that his brother packed into the raft is properly secured, "and I'll navigate around the worst parts, this trip is about speed and staying dry. No one's paying me to scare the shit out of them today. OK?"

All I have to do is sit in the boat and not fall out. Right. Check. Good to know we have the same plan.

After securing the gear-- and me-- I watch him jog up to touch base with his parents one more time. Annie and Vera take turns hugging him and I see Rapid punch him in the arm before his dad pats him on the back.

My gut clenches. This family is everything mine wasn't and seeing the way they love and support each other makes me yearn for something I'm not sure I'm ever going to find now.

"OK." River lands in the raft with a running start, pushing us off short and into the water with one foot before pulling himself all the way in and grabbing the oar. "You have two hours to fall madly in love with me. I need to know everything about you, starting with how the fuck you know the Everly Brothers."

Rocklyn Ryder

River

"How do *you* know the Everly Brothers?" She shoots back at me; her hand is still white-knuckling the handle beside her but at least she's laughing.

"Have you met Don and Vera?" I reply, giving her a grin. "I know more shit from the sixties than I do from my own generation. "When I was a kid, thought Vera made up all the songs she sang all the time. The first time I heard Take Me Home, Country Roads, I thought John Denver ripped off my grandma's song."

Cinnamon's laughing at my story, relaxing enough to let go of the grab handle even.

"Vera didn't play records or tapes? Didn't you ever listen to the radio?" She asks, wiping a tear from the corner of her eye.

"It was the nineties," I point out. "Not a lot of radio stations were still playing John Denver."

I tell her more about growing up. What it was like having three older brothers, what it's like having parents that are still together-- and won't shut up about it.

Being part of a close family, growing up in a tight-knit community like Moonshine Ridge. The pros and the cons of living in such a small town.

Cinnamon can't get enough of my family stories and I'll tell them all to her eventually, but I meant it when I said I wanted to know everything about her and she keeps ducking my questions every time I try to steer the conversation back to her.

"My mom had some-- issues," she tells me. "So, I spent most of my time at nana's apartment when I was growing up. Nana was born in the late sixties so she knew all those eighties songs and loved to show me pictures of herself from when she was a teenager, but she always said she was born too late. She really loved all the oldies music and that's how I know the Everly Brothers.

"She used to put on records that had been her mom's and we would sing to them all day long."

"So, you don't have any brothers or sisters? It was just you and your grandmother?"

"Only child," she confirms. "Mom met a guy when I was in high school. Jimmy."

Her eyes go distant and her voice chokes on his name and I know there's a dark story there. My mind is going in all the usual directions and I'm thinking about ways to kill the guy but then she says he was good to them in a way that makes me think I'm reading things wrong.

"If this Jimmy guy was so good to you guys, how come you say his name like you just took a shot of battery acid?"

"Oh. Um. Nothing like you're probably thinking. He was a pretty good guy, really. He took care of my mom when she got cancer and even after she passed away, he sent me money every month so I could afford to share a place with some friends while I went to community college and I only had to work part time. It's just...maybe he wasn't that bright, I guess."

"College? What are you studying?"

I use the edge of the paddle to push us to the side of the river where the water is flowing fast but calm but I'm too caught up in Cin's story and I make the move too late to avoid all the faster water.

The raft bounces over some mild rapids before I can get us back on flat water. Cinnamon's hand wraps around the handle again but then she grins.

"That was kinda fun," she tells me. Her story is lost in her enjoyment of my river and all the questions I had been planning to ask are forgotten in watching her smile.

Chapter Five

Cinnamon

River's too easy to talk to, before I know it, I'm telling him more about myself than I'd planned to.

I can't believe I'm even thinking about telling him what happened-- after Mom passed away. Why Jimmy's a bad memory now. Why everything is a bad memory.

Then we go over some little waves in the river that make the whole raft bounce under me and it's actually fun. I'm laughing and I'm about to ask if we can do it again when a flash lights up the walls of the steep canyon we're in. River's expression hardens and when thunder rolls overhead he shakes his head like he's annoyed.

"Change of plans, honey," he says. He drops the

oar into the water and I watch the way his muscles strain against the effort as he uses the broad side of the blade to change our course in a dramatic turn that sends us directly to a small beach where the river bends along one shore.

Storm clouds that had still been far on the horizon when we left camp seem to have caught up to us in record time. Another flash lights up the sky and this time I hear River counting quietly to himself as he helps me out of the raft and onto the beach.

"Fuck," he mutters when the thunder crashes at the count of twenty.

I help him pull the raft all the way out of the water and he uses a rope to tie it to a tree near the clearing.

"That's too close," he tells me. "Do me a favor, grab that bag and yours and head over there, OK? I'll be right there."

I unfasten the strap and lift the bag he pointed to out of the raft, then I look for my bag, but I don't have a bag. Am I supposed to have a bag? No one told me to pack anything. I didn't even have a chance.

River is standing on the little beach with something in his hand. Then he looks up at the clouds that are quickly covering the bright blue we'd been enjoying.

"OK, I got a message through so they know we're

OK. Search and Rescue isn't going to waste time and money trying to find us, but it's a good bet that we're stuck here over night."

He's rattling off information in a no-nonsense tone, taking the pack from my hands and digging through it.

If I thought laid-back, joking-around River was hot; serious, take-charge River has the last of my defenses waving a white flag.

He finds a spot that he says will be safe from the storm and sets up a tiny little tent.

"It's a two-person tent, but it's going to be a tight fit. Or do you have your own?"

"I don't have anything," I confess.

River stops and looks at me. I must look pathetic. I feel so helpless and stupid.

"They didn't give you an emergency dry bag?"

He comes to stand in front of me, his deep blue eyes narrowed at me in concern. I shake my head.

"That storm is moving faster than we calculated. We can't be on the water when there's lightning activity this close."

I nod my head up and down. Got it. Storm. Lightning plus water equals dead. This is a concept I can understand very easily.

"We only have one bag with emergency gear in it," he continues. "One shelter--" he turns and points back at the little tent, "-- and one sleeping bag."

"Oh," I understand the problem. "It's OK, I can just--"

"The fuck you can!" He cuts me off, sliding his hand up my bare arms and holding me in place. "The temps are going to drop fast once the rain reaches us. I know you're thinking it's summer and it's still warm but hypothermia can set in even at these temperatures.

"Listen to me, Cinnamon, there are two things that I am not taking any risk with, this storm and my woman. Understand?"

His what?

I nod dumbly as the first fat drops of rain start to fall.

"Honey, I'd love to be a gentleman and let you have the sleeping bag to yourself, but in this situation that's not chivalry, that's a death wish. We're going to have to share."

River

It's torture. Plain and simple torture, and even though it's killing me to feel Cinnamon's sweet curves pressed against me, I wouldn't trade it for the world.

Problem is, I'm rock fucking hard and there's not a damn thing I can do to hide it from her.

It's an extra-large sleeping bag. At six, three and wide in the shoulders, it's hard to find lightweight sleeping bags that I fit into. So, this one's pretty bulky.

I added a Mylar emergency blanket under the inflatable pad to help retain some heat and unzipped the sleeping bag to give us the most space possible, but the tent is just an emergency pup tent. Even if Cinnamon had her own sleeping bag, we'd still close enough that we'd practically be on top of each other.

On top of each other is exactly how I'd rather we were spending the night; but as bad as I want to claim this treasure and finally make her mine, I know the whole day has been a lot for her. I don't want her to think I'm trying take advantage of her in the situation.

I was able to get some hot soup in both of us before it got too bad outside. At least we're not going to sleep with empty stomachs.

"So, you have signal to text up here?"

Cinnamon's body is pressed to mine while I lay awkwardly on my back, doing my best to keep my hard-on to myself. She's curled halfway toward me and I'd give anything to put my arm around her and feel her head resting on my chest.

"We have satellite communications," I explain, "they have emergency locators on them but they can send and receive simple texts. So yeah, I was able to let them know we got caught up river and we're OK."

The dark green walls of the thin, nylon tent light up and thunder crashes overhead.

Cinnamon's body presses closer to mine. Her head finds the crook of my shoulder and her arm wraps across my chest tightly.

"Scared of storms?" I ask, wrapping my arm around her trembling body and holding her tightly against me while I take a deep, deliberate breath to keep myself from rolling over and letting her feel my need for her.

"Not usually," she giggles softly and I can feel her breath hot through the layers of my t-shirt and hoodie. "I've never actually camped out in one before. Actually, I've never actually camped out at all before coming to work for your parents."

"We're OK here," I assure her, taking full advantage of the chance to hold her close like this, "we're off the water, we're sheltered, the storm is just a lot of noise and light but it's going to go right over us."

"I trust you," she says. "I feel safe with you."

She moves closer still, bending a knee and moving her leg over mine. Before I can move, her thigh makes contact with the steel rod under my sweat pants, sending stars exploding in my vision.

"Is that because of me?"

Her voice is soft and shy, sounding as if she's genuinely unsure.

All I can do is groan in answer, tightening my arm around her as she moves her hand back across over my chest.

"All you, honey," I grit out.

After an agonizing silence where I don't know if I've freaked her out or what, she lifts her head slightly and I can feel her eyes on me in the darkness.

"Is it because of *me*, or just because I'm female?"

This game is over. I'm not playing the nice guy anymore. Cinnamon needs to know she's mine and now is my chance to show her.

I turn on my side so I'm facing her and place her hand over my throbbing erection.

"You, honey girl," I tell her. "Only you. Always you."

It's too dark to see but I can feel her eyes on me as she presses her hand against me, exploring through my clothes with shy fingers.

"Earlier," she whispers, "outside, you called me yours..."

My lips find hers and seal off her next words. Silencing the uncertainty in her tone, I make sure she understands what I meant.

Chapter Six

Cinnamon

His kiss catches me off guard.

My heart is already beating so loudly I can't hear the storm around us over the sound of it, and now River's lips are on mine and I can't hear anything. It's like my brain can't keep my other senses online anymore, I'm too overwhelmed by the feel of him against me.

His body turns toward me, lining up against mine so that I feel that hard rod digging into the space between my thighs. His arms are wrapped around me, holding me prisoner against his solid chest as his mouth claims mine.

I haven't kissed many boys and I've never been kissed like this. River's tongue coaxing mine into a heated tangle is the reason that kissing exists.

My hand stays between us, taking advantage of the opportunity to explore his hardness. My fingers wrap around his girth, feeling the way it jumps and pulses through the fabric of his sweats and taking note of every way I can touch him that makes him grind into my grip or growl deep in his throat between our kisses.

I've never touched a man this way before and I love the way River's reaction makes me feel empowered. But also, my body responds to his every move, his every touch; every sound he makes has me breathless and needy and I know he's the only man that will ever be able to make this ache subside.

When our kisses grow less desperate and deepen to something more intimate, his hand reaches up and traces the side of my face. Then down my body, taking its time to truly feel all my curves as his fingers bring goosebumps to my skin.

He kneads my breasts, pushing his hand under my shirt and running the pad of his thumb over my sensitive nipples, making me moan.

Then his hand trails lower, making my entire body tremble in anticipation as his fingers breach the waistband of the borrowed sweats from his stash of emergency gear.

"Damn, you're wet." His mouth whispers against my ear as his fingers make their way between my legs, stroking my hot center through my soaked panties.

"Because of you," I whisper back, raising my knee over his leg to open up more space for his fingers to move in strong strokes that have me growing more and more frustrated with the layers of clothing between us.

Like he can read my mind, River tugs at my pants and then my panties. The two of us moving awkwardly in the tight space of the little shelter till I'm naked from the waist down with River bent between my knees.

"Not fucking fair." I hear him growl.

We're both pretzeled around each other, trying to stay within the confines of the tent. River's knees are between mine, his fingers dragging through my slick folds while I writhe against his touch.

"I want to taste you so fucking bad," he rasps out, but there's not enough room for him to wedge his bulky frame in the space we have to work with.

In frustration, he covers me instead, kissing me again while he pushes his thick erection against my mound and moves against me like he's desperate to scratch an itch.

And I have the same itch.

One of my hands is clinging to his back while I drive the other under the fabric of the last layer still between us.

There's nothing under his sweatpants but him. Hot skin, and hardness. My hand wraps around his shaft and I'm fascinated at how hard he is. Wet pre-cum oozes from the tip and I'm overwhelmed with the desire to taste him too.

His hands are under my shirt and on my breasts, and then my shirt is over my head and shoved aside while he uses his mouth to tease each one of my nipples into stiff peaks.

I push his pants off his hips, needing better access to tough him, to give him better access to press himself against me.

If it's still storming outside, I can't hear it. If it's cold, I don't feel it. Inside our thin, nylon tent, I'm burning for this man. All my better judgment has been drowned in the river rushing near our secluded little beach.

When he's naked against me, I instinctively move so that my legs are open wide to make room for him to settle between them; but when he drags the broad tip of his dick along my seam, I have to tell him.

"River." I can barely speak. His name comes out on a gasp as another stroke of his manhood contacts my clit and sends sparks cascading through me. I'm aching and needy and I've never felt so empty like this.

I want to feel him inside me, filling me up, and making me whole.

"I'm not on birth control," I warn him, "I've-- I've never actually done this before."

His forehead drops to mine and, with his lips nearly touching mine, he whispers. "Me either...and I don't care."

River

I hold my breath and wait. If Cinnamon wants to stop now, I might die, but I'll understand.

I've taken her from telling me I'm off limits to begging for my cock in a matter of weeks and maybe these aren't the ideal circumstances to be asking her to make this decision.

She's still a virgin and I'm an asshole for wanting to change that right now.

It's my first time too, but there hasn't been a shred of doubt in my mind that Cinnamon and I are meant for each other since I first laid eyes on her. I've been ready to give myself to her in every way since that first day.

"You either what?"

My eyes have long since adjusted to the darkness and I can see her blink up at me when she says it.

"I've never done this either, honey," I clarify. "You're going to be my first, Cin. You're going to be my *only*."

There's not a damn stitch of clothing left

between us and the nylon walls of the little emergency tent are coated with condensation from our heavy breathing.

Cinnamon's arm moves, sending a spray of drops falling over us.

"I don't understand," she says, "how? How could you possibly still be a virgin?"

I laugh and kiss her again. She tastes delicious and I'm disappointed that our cramped quarters don't give me a chance to touch her and taste her in all the ways I want to, but there's gonna be plenty of time for that when this group has gone home and I can get her to my cabin for a few days.

"You've heard my folks tell their story," I tell her softly, laying more kisses on her sweet lips, "I've always known it was going to be like that for me too. That one day I was going to meet a girl and I was going to know she was the one. I didn't want to waste time on something I knew wasn't real."

"And you think I'm--"

I cut her off with a deep kiss, swallowing the words she was about to say and letting my body answer her.

My cock is so hard it's throbbing, and pre-cum is leaking from the tip, mixing with her own juices as I rub myself against her.

"Look, I don't give a fuck if we use birth control or not, Cinnamon. I want you forever. I'm planning on making you my wife and filling you with my babies anyway. It doesn't matter to me if you get pregnant our first time or our four hundredth."

Cin wiggles under me and the little whimper that comes out of her throat is fucking adorable. I know she likes what I'm saying.

I take one hand and draw my fingertips along her skin on my way down till I'm reaching between us. I have to give myself room to touch her with my hand and losing the heat of her core pressed against my dick is physically painful, but I slide my fingers along her seam. She's so fucking wet and ready, it's easy for me to press two fingers through her opening and sink them deep inside her.

"If you want to wait--" I pant, clenching my jaw to keep from coming before I'm inside her. The feel of her velvet tunnel clenching against my fingers as I search for the spot I know is there, has me so far gone I'm on the edge of not being able to keep the promise I'm about to make.

"-- I can make you feel good, honey." I feel the spot I'm looking for and rub my fingertip against it.

Cinnamon's eyes widen and her hands grip my biceps, digging short nails into my skin, and I fucking love it. I love feeling her hips buck up against mine and the way the walls of her channel flex against my fingers as she pants underneath me.

"I'll spend all night making you come for me," I

tell her, moving my thumb over her swollen clit and making good on my promise.

Cinnamon's body spasms, her moans becoming hoarse cries that join the howling winds overhead while I work my hand against her secret places till she comes so beautifully for me that I'm biting the inside of my lip to keep me from joining her.

"Fuck me." She's begging as soon as she can breathe again. Her hands are on my ass, and her knees are open wide. "Do it, River, take me. Make me yours. I need you inside me."

Without hesitation, I'm obeying her commands. I line my dick up against her opening and push forward.

My heart's pounding, adrenaline pouring into my bloodstream, and I'm trying so hard to think of anything but how fucking amazing her pussy feels as I enter her.

If I hurt her, she doesn't let on. There's only Cinnamon's soft mewling, begging for more as I inch deeper inside her tightness until there's only one thing left to fill her with. That thought has me drawing back and thrusting forward, hard this time.

Cinnamon grunts softly as I bottom out before thrusting into her willing body in fast, hard strokes. Sweat pools on my skin as I concentrate on making this last. It feels too fucking good for it to be over yet, but I can already feel my balls tightening.

"Come for me one more time, honey," I demand

from her, flicking my thumb over her clit again and combining the motion with my thrusts till I've got her wound up so tight she's about to go off like a rocket for me again.

"River," she grasps at my back, clamping her thighs around my hips and meeting each of my strokes with her hips. "I'm going to come."

I can feel it. I can feel her pussy getting greedy for my come; clenching tight and milking my dick, begging to pull my seed deep inside her womb so it'll take root there and that's the last thought left in my brain as I give in.

Cinnamon's grinding against me, her body shuddering in her own release as I pump everything I've been holding onto for all these years into her.

The storm has moved on. I can still hear the winds and the thunder off in the distance, but there's a peaceful calm that's settled around the small space we're camped in.

The rush of the river provides its comforting sound to the quiet between us.

Reaching over to fumble through my things, I find a cloth and use it clean us both up.

"That was better than I expected it to be," Cinnamon confesses sleepily as I gather her into my arms, pulling her against me and loving the feel of her head resting against my chest.

"Fuck yeah it was." I sigh and kiss the top of her head.

Her breathing is already deep and even and I can feel sleep pulling me into the same peaceful oblivion.

She's mine, I think with a smile, as I hold my woman in my arms and drift off.

Chapter Seven

Cinnamon

Dawn lights up the little tent early, waking us both up.

The storm is long gone but River's in no hurry to pack up and get back to camp.

Before bothering to find our clothes or greet the day, we make love again. This time more slowly, quieter, taking our time to learn more about one another and how to make it feel even better.

But we can't stay here forever.

As we pack up and enjoy cups of coffee that River brewed in the tiny camp kettle, an incoming message on his satellite communicator breaks the spell, reminding me that I've been living in a fantasy for the last twenty-four hours.

River has spent the morning living up to everything he said in the heat of the moment last night. Acting like we're a couple now and talking about the future he has planned for us.

"I need to tell you something."

He's singing Stick With Me, Baby-- the old Everly Brothers song we sang together by the fire just a couple of night ago.

I've been thinking of it as our song ever since, and now I know he does too.

"Tell me anything," he says, taking me in his arms and kissing me before standing back up to his full height and grinning down at me.

"River-- I don't know if your parents are going to approve of us."

"Mom and Dad love you, Cin," he assures me, looking at me confused. "Don and Vera love you, my brothers-- even Jackson thinks you're cool. Why wouldn't they approve?"

I try to wriggle out of his arms but he pins me tighter.

"Honey, what's up?" He asks seriously.

"I went to prison." I blurt it out, there's no other way to say it. "My mom and her boyfriend were growing weed on their land when Mom passed away."

River doesn't loosen his grip around me, but he pulls his head back to give me a hard stare.

"Jimmy owed back taxes or something so they bought the land in Mom's name only," I explain.

"When she died, Jimmy kept farming. When he got busted..."

"Shh, hey." River's finger wipes a tear off my cheek. "Cin, honey, it's just pot. I don't get it?"

I explain the details. How I got caught up in the case, getting held accountable because I'd technically inherited the land.

"But isn't it's legal there, what's the big deal?" River has a rock to lean against, pulling my back to his chest and cradling me against him.

I explain that I was barely nineteen when Jimmy got busted, how the DA wasn't convinced I didn't know about it because I'd accepted cash from Jimmy and Mom when they moved and because Jimmy had continued to send money to help me out with rent and college even after Mom passed away from cancer.

"Legal is a pretty big gray area," I tell River, "there are a ton of really strict rules for growing, and Jimmy wasn't following any of them.

"My public defender was able to negotiate less jail time for me, but I still spent eighteen months in prison. I have a felony record. I lost everything-- my friends drifted off. I had to drop out of my classes, and when I got out, my job wouldn't hire me back...in fact, no one would hire me.

"That's how I ended up working for your family. Bank and Annie were the only ones who were willing to give me a second chance."

I spin around to face him, fear taking hold in my gut.

"They aren't going to want their baby boy dating a criminal," I tell him, "and I need their reference so I can get another job when I leave Moonshine Ridge."

"What happened to Jimmy?"

Shrugging my shoulders, I tell him no one knows. "He skipped bail and no one's heard from him since. I don't even know if he knows I went to jail."

"That is a special kind of fucked up, honey."

"Yeah well, you know what they say, no one will fuck you like family."

His arms circle my waist again and he draws me close so I'm standing between his knees. With him still leaning on the boulder, we're face to face.

"Sounds like you need a new family," he tells me with a half-grin.

River is taking this news in stride and I can't help but relax a little that he's not freaking out the way my old roommates did before they cut me out of their lives.

"Yeah, well, it's not like I can just order one of those off the internet, you know."

River

D amn. That's a hell of a story. No wonder Cinnamon's been fighting to keep her distance all this time.

I've got a lot of questions, sure, but the most important thing right now is making sure my girl knows that this is not a deal breaker. Far damn from it, in fact. And I can guarantee that my folks don't give a rat's ass about her record either.

"Well, I hear them Joneses up in Moonshine Ridge are pretty decent folk," I tease. "Kinda crazy, but good people. Maybe you could talk to one of them about giving you a new name?"

"River Jones, are you asking me to marry you?" She laughs, wiping a new tear off her cheek and blushing that pretty scarlet color that makes her skin glow.

"Hell yeah, I am," I pull her close and kiss her hard. "I told you; I knew you were the one the moment I saw you."

I'll be getting down on one knee and doing this right another time, but right now we need to catch up with the rest of the group and I can't let Cinnamon leave this spot till she understands that she's mine. We're in this together now and we'll find our way just like the song says.

"That's crazy, River," she tells me. But she's laughing and her eyes are shining with hope for our future.

"That's the way mountain men do it, honey," I tell her.

"I knew too," she whispers, leaning in to touch her lips to mine, "I knew it was going to be you."

"Then we'd better get back to the group so we can let Mom and Vera know there's going to be two more places at the couples table for the reception."

It's fucking hard to stop kissing her. I want to spread the sleeping bag back out and lay her down again. I want to spin her around and bend her over the rock I'm sitting on. I want to stay right here and have her ride my swollen cock cowgirl style till neither one of us can think straight anymore. But the damn satellite device pings with a new message and I have to take solace in knowing that I've got the rest of my life to please this angel in every way possible.

"What reception?" Cin asks as she helps me strap gear back into the raft.

"My brothers all got married in the last twelve months," I explain. "None of them bothered having weddings, either, they all skipped down to Slow River and got hitched at the courthouse. Mom and Vera have been planning a big, group reception to celebrate this September, when the river season ends, and before the snow starts falling so it doesn't interfere with Eddy and Pepper's ski season up at the lodge they own."

Running to the Mountain

"Is that what Rapid keeps giving you shit about? The party you're not invited to?"

I can't help but laugh. All my brothers have been razzing me and I'm looking forward to rubbing their noses in it when I get my ring on Cinnamon's finger official-like.

"That'd be it."

I double check our camp, making sure nothing got left behind...except for a couple of V-cards that neither of us are going to be needing again anyway.

Helping to get Cinnamon situated in the raft, I push us off the sandy little beach and into the water, jumping in just before the boat gets caught by the current.

"Hey," I tell her, loving that she's sitting relaxed and comfy and not nervous about the river anymore, "what do you say we see their reception and raise them a wedding?"

"You mean, get married at the big party? In September?"

She grabs the extra paddle and follows my lead, learning how to help steer and keep us headed down river.

"If you're willing to wait that long, yeah."

Cinnamon blushes that pretty shade for me again and I know the next time I ask her to go for a walk after camp clean up, she'll be taking me up on it.

"As long as we don't have to wait that long for anything else, I guess."

There's another little beach on the river bank up ahead and I dig my paddle in to the current to steer us toward it.

We'll be a little later than I'd told Rapid to expect us in. I'm not making my girl wait another minute for what she's hinting at.

Epilogue 1
3 months later

Cinnamon

The minister pronounces us man and wife and tells River he can kiss his bride.

Thank goodness we're having an informal, old-fashioned, mountain wedding in the big barn on the Jones family property called Riverbend. If we were in a church, we'd probably be getting kicked out, because the way River kisses me is anything but church appropriate!

We come up for air to the sounds of most of Moonshine Ridge whistling and cat-calling us and the very distinctive voice of River's oldest brother, Rapid, yelling at us to "get a room."

The party started before noon today, while me and my new sisters-in-law were still helping Vera and Annie with last minute decorations and set up:

the music's been playing all day, there's been an endless supply of snacks and Ginger and Current brought plenty of beer from their brewery in town to keep anyone from driving home tonight, no matter how late they stay.

To make sure no one was too sloshed before the "I Dos," I walked down the aisle at one p.m. Twenty minutes later, I'm officially Mrs. River Jones, jogging hand in hand with my husband down a gauntlet of flying bird seed and confetti as we make our way directly to the dance floor.

River and I agreed to do it up right today, making sure someone in his family has a full-blown wedding.

It turns out that River's brothers and parents aren't the only ones who skipped the traditional fanfare-- over the last few months I also found out that Vera and Don did their vows Vegas style back in the early sixties when they were touring the country in their converted school bus.

River looks like he belongs on the red carpet at the Oscars in his classic, black tuxedo and I feel like a princess with the train of my floor length gown sweeping the floor behind me.

The room goes silent around us as I gather the train and hook the little loop over my wrist so I don't trip over it.

We'll be changing before things get too far along and I'm looking forward to getting some time alone with my husband, but first, we're on the hook for a dance.

Friends and family gather at the edges of the dance floor as the DJ cues our song.

River takes one of my hands in his and slips his other hand around me to the back of my waist, and pulls me close as the first notes of Stick With Me, Baby fill the big barn through the sound system.

It's not the Everly Brothers. When we were going through music for our portion of tonight's playlist, we found this version and fell in love with its lilting, sentimental style.

"You are absolutely stunning, Mrs. Jones," River tells me as he guides me over the floor, every bit as talented at dancing as he is at everything else.

"Wait till you see what's under the dress." I wink at him, loving the way his eyes darken as they graze downward over my body.

We practiced our dance. Nothing fancy, but we weren't planning on standing in the middle of the floor swaying gently to the music-- but that's what happens anyway.

Epilogue 2
5 years later

River

I've been waiting all week for the official documents to get delivered.

This has been a busy year for Cinnamon and I; our son, Reed, was born in February, we officially took over the rafting business at the end of the season in September when my parents decided to retire-- sorta, and thanks to the paperwork I'm carrying across the property right now, my wife is no longer an ex-con.

Not that I give a fuck.

Cinnamon's past hasn't impacted us at all. It sure as hell hasn't made me love her any less. No one in the family cares and no one else in Moonshine Ridge knows.

"Hey honey," I find her over at Rapid and Sage's place, standing in the kitchen with Sage while our four-year-old daughter, Fennel, plays in the living room with my niece, Basil.

Cin blushes when I catch her lips in a kiss that's more than she was expecting.

My sister-in-law rolls her eyes but doesn't say anything. Doc can't talk, her and Rapid are just as bad most of the time.

"What's this?" Cinnamon asks as I hand her the cardboard shipping envelope.

"I think it's what we've been waiting for," I tell her, eager for her to open it.

When she sees the return address, her hands start to shake.

"Oh my gosh," she mumbles under her breath as she rips it open. "I can't believe it."

"Is that what I think it is?" Sage asks from the other side of the kitchen island.

Cinnamon's eyes tear up as she sorts through the papers that she spreads out on the island counter top.

Nodding, she answers Sage, "Yep, I'm not a felon anymore."

"Congratulations!" Sage comes around and gives Cinnamon a hug. "Welcome to the world of voting rights."

It took a lot of patience, and a pricey attorney,

but we were able to get Cinnamon's record expunged.

"Yup, now Vera's the only criminal in the family," I joke.

My grandmother and her friends are still terrorizing the Ridge. We got a call from Deputy Hawkins to come pick her up from the station again just last week. We keep waiting for her and her friends to get too old to cause trouble, but instead it seems they get worse every year.

"Let's go home and celebrate," I whisper in my wife's ear.

"Go!" Sage waves her hands at us to shoo us out of the house, "Rapid and I can watch the kids for a while. This is something that calls for some grown-up time."

"We're getting grown-up time?" Rapid's voice butts in as he joins us in the kitchen, bending in to kiss his wife and not-so-sneakily cop a feel of her backside.

"We're babysitting," she laughs as she swats my brother's hand off her bottom, "River and Cinnamon need to do some celebrating tonight."

When Rapid sees the paperwork on the counter he gives us a nod.

"You owe me, little brother," he tells me while Cinnamon and I say good bye to the kids, and I know what he means, since he and Sage have two little ones of their own now too, in addition to Sage's teenage son who's at an age where he wants to spend more time with his buddies than his parents.

I'm sure it won't be long before he comes around to collect on that, but right now I have a few hours to have my wife all to myself and I plan on taking advantage of every minute.

Thank you for Reading

I hoped you enjoyed meeting the Jones family and following each of the brothers to their happily ever after!

If you're curious about the songs mentioned, River and Cinnamon's song is "Stick With Me, Baby," by the Everly Brothers but the version they play at their wedding is the cover by Robert Plant and Allison Krauss.

The John Prine song they sing in Rapid and Sage's final epilogue is Spanish Pipedream and I mentioned Moonshadow by Cat Stevens and some Bob Marley songs in Current and Ginger's book.

All the Jones boys except River are tone deaf— like their author— and should not be encouraged to sing in public spaces!

FUN FACT: I learned Moonshadow at Girlscout camp a *very* long time ago.

Thanks for reading!
Rocklyn

Next from the Moonshine Ridge Mountain Men

The Diaz family:

Meet the Diaz family, beginning with
Mountain Man's Offer
Vale Diaz

Rocklyn Ryder

The pretty, young thing pouring my whiskey today is new around here. One look and immediately I'm a man obsessed. But Sparrow doesn't need a grumpy, ex-Marine hovering over her. The Corps left me with too many scars; both the kind that show and the kind that don't, for me to think this ray of sunshine would have anything to do with the likes of me.

Until some pencil-neck weasel comes into the bar one night while I'm nursing a drink I only ordered so I could see Sparrow.

He wants her back; orders her to walk off her job and come home with him this instant.

That's when I stand up, using all six foot, five inches of my wide frame to tell the nitwit to leave my fiancé alone.

Now Sparrow's stuck with me, pretending I'm the love of her life while we wait her ex to give up and leave town without her.

But when our little charade crosses the line, I only have one chance to convince her that I'm not pretending.

About the Author

Rocklyn prefers her romance reads to be short, cute, and dirty; low drama and a little over-the-top: extra points for growly, alpha heroes with beards.

Originally from the farms and ranches of Central California, Rocklyn grew up in the lap of the Sierra Nevada mountains. Those small towns will always be home, but Rocklyn was born to roam.

These days she spends her days exploring America's back roads in her camper trailer, writing steamy happily-ever-afters while looking for internet.

Keep in touch when you join her (mostly) weekly newsletter and never miss updates on what she has in the works-- and what's working and not in a life full of adventure and shenanigans.

Sign up here or by visiting Rocklyn online at https://www.rocklynwrites.net

Printed in Dunstable, United Kingdom